////////NASCAR.

FULLY ENGAGED

Abby Gaines

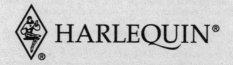

HARLEQUIN®

TORONTO • NEW YORK • LONDON
AMSTERDAM • PARIS • SYDNEY • HAMBURG
STOCKHOLM • ATHENS • TOKYO • MILAN • MADRID
PRAGUE • WARSAW • BUDAPEST • AUCKLAND

ISBN-13: 978-0-373-21787-8
ISBN-10: 0-373-21787-0

FULLY ENGAGED

SECRETS and **LEGENDS**

FULLY ENGAGED
by Abby Gaines

From the opening green flag at Daytona to the final
checkered flag at Homestead, the competition will be
fierce for the NASCAR Sprint Cup Series championship.

The **Grosso** family practically has engine oil in their veins. For
them racing represents not just a way of life but a tradition that
goes back to NASCAR's inception. Like all families, they also
have a few skeletons to hide. What happens when someone
peeks inside the closet becomes a matter that threatens to
destroy them.

The **Murphys** have been supporting drivers in the pits for
generations, despite a vendetta with the Grossos that's almost as
old as NASCAR itself! But the Murphys have their own secrets...
and a few indiscretions that could cost them everything.

The **Branches** are newcomers, and some would say upstarts.
But as this affluent Texas family is further enmeshed in the world
of NASCAR, they become just as embroiled in the intrigues on
and off the track.

The **Motor Media Group** are the PR people responsible for the
positive public perception of NASCAR's stars. They are the glue
that repairs the damage. And more than anything, they feel the
brunt of the backlash....

These NASCAR families have secrets to hide, and reputations to
protect. This season will test them all.

Dear Reader,

Writing a book that's part of a series of linked stories has been a new experience for me—so I'm as excited as any reader to see the stories that will unfold throughout this year in NASCAR: SECRETS AND LEGENDS.

In *Fully Engaged* you'll meet disillusioned team owner Gideon Taney, a guy who's had enough of NASCAR and wants out. His attitude is a problem for Sandra Jacobs, whose business—and personal—survival depends on Gideon's investment in the sport. Is there any chance she can change the mind of a man as decisive, forceful—and just plain bossy—as Gideon Taney?

I'd love to know if you enjoy this story. Please e-mail me at abby@abbygaines.com. And if, like me, you hate to say goodbye to characters at the end of a book, visit the For Readers page at www.abbygaines.com, where you'll find some extra "After the End" scenes for *Fully Engaged,* including Gideon and Sandra's wedding day.

Sincerely,

Abby Gaines

ABBY GAINES

Like some of her favorite NASCAR drivers, Abby Gaines's first love was open-wheel dirt track racing. But the lure of NASCAR—the speed, the power, the awesome scale—proved irresistible, just as it did for those drivers. Now Abby is thrilled to be combining her love of NASCAR with her love of writing.

When she's not writing romance novels for Harlequin's officially licensed NASCAR series and for Harlequin Superromance, Abby works as editor of a speedway magazine. She lives with her husband and three children, just a short drive from her favorite dirt track.

Abby's next book is *The Diaper Diaries,* out in March 2008 from Harlequin Superromance. Visit Abby at www.abbygaines.com, or e-mail her at abby@abbygaines.com.

For Nicole, patient reader and best-ever sister, with love

When her father skips the country with embezzled funds, Penny Branch and her family struggle to stay afloat. The only good news to come out of the Branch family debacle is that Penny has reunited with her estranged husband, executive Craig Lockhart. But how will the rest of the family survive?

CHAPTER ONE

THE CLOCK ON THE WALL of the TV studio's greenroom showed 6:55 a.m.—time for Sandra Jacobs to pour herself a third cup of coffee. Time to panic.

As she refilled her cup from the pot supplied by one of the *Olivia Winton Show*'s many minions, Sandra's stomach growled a reminder that she hadn't had breakfast. She told her hips to be grateful, and took a scalding sip of the too-hot coffee to settle her stomach. Was it possible to feel both panicked and hungry? By rights, she felt the two shouldn't go together.

"Come on, guys, where are you?" she muttered as she resumed her pacing of the room. She'd set up the media coup of her career, and so far, she was the only person here to witness it. So much for her plan to impress the heck out of her client, Gideon Taney, the notoriously unimpressable boss of Taney Motorsports. Taney, as he was known to everyone, hadn't bothered to show up. Which might not be a bad thing, considering his NASCAR Sprint Cup Series driver, Will Branch, the show's guest of honor, hadn't arrived, either.

The clock's unnaturally loud *tick-tick* marked the inexorable progress of Will's tardiness from inconvenience to potential disaster. Sandra couldn't afford to screw up in front of Taney. Not when another clock—the countdown on her business loan repayments—ticked constantly in the back of her mind.

The greenroom, where studio guests waited with their hangers-on, had no window to the outside, so Sandra couldn't tell if some freakish Chicago storm had held everyone up. But it had been fine, if dark, when she'd left her hotel earlier.

Behind her, the door opened and Sandra spun around, sloshing hot coffee over the rim of the mug onto her thumb. "Ouch! Where have you—" halfway through, she realized the new arrival wasn't Will Branch, the AWOL driver, and she tailed off like a winding-down action toy "—been?"

"All your life?" Gideon Taney completed her question as he strode into the room, six foot four of dark-haired, dark-eyed, I'm-the-boss-and-don't-you-forget-it masculinity.

Which, as always, started another little *tick-tick* inside Sandra. She figured Taney's brand of solid strength and sharp intelligence resonated in some primitive place inside all women, causing their biological clocks—*everyone's, not just mine*—to tick louder when he was around. He was the kind of perfect specimen of manhood that scientists would choose to procreate the species. She could imagine, after a nuclear holocaust, men like Gideon Taney being rounded up and kept in some top-secret, radiation-free zone, where they would be charged with rebuilding humankind.

As if Taney would allow himself to be rounded up!

She dropped her frivolous theories about human survival and focused on the hint of a smile that pulled Taney's mouth out of its usual straight line. And there was that little quip he'd just made. *Someone's in a good mood.* She might need that. But her own mood wasn't so great, and she sounded ungracious when she said, "I thought you were Will."

Taney's gaze sharpened. "He's not here?" The censure in his deep voice implied it was Sandra's fault.

"There's plenty of time." If you called half an hour plenty. She put down her coffee, grabbed a paper napkin, wiped her thumb. "He knows how important this is for him."

Will Branch's appearance on the *Olivia Winton Show,* America's most popular breakfast TV show, was even more important for Sandra.

She'd pulled every string, called in every favor anyone had ever owed her. She'd spent hours on the phone, she'd e-mailed, she'd sent autographed NASCAR memorabilia to anyone at the studio whose second cousin's stepdaughter's nephew was a fan. All to secure this coveted spot.

"You do realize," she told Taney, because a P.R. consultant whose business teetered on the brink of financial extinction couldn't afford to be shy of blowing her own trumpet, "Olivia hasn't interviewed a NASCAR driver before? For Will to get in first, when he's never even won a race…"

And when he'd got a DNF—Did Not Finish—in Martinsville on Sunday, as if he were determined to make her job impossible. He had made it to third place before he'd blown a tire, but Sandra wasn't convinced he'd have sustained that performance, even on four good tires.

"The other team owners will turn green over their cereal," Taney said drily.

"You could just admit I've done a great job." Plain speaking tended to work best with the man.

He raised an eyebrow. "You know that if I give you the least encouragement you'll put up your fees." He sat down on the beige leather couch, long legs stretched out in front of him, hands clasped behind his head. The beautifully tailored sports jacket that sheathed his powerful shoulders parted to hint at a broad chest beneath the dark polo shirt. Sandra was tall, and she liked to think she cut a striking figure, but Taney had Presence. Sitting didn't dissipate that Presence one iota.

Since his comment about an increase in fees was uncannily accurate, she chose not to answer. "Any progress on finding a new sponsor for Will?"

They desperately needed to sign a new primary sponsor, and Will's appearance with Olivia Winton would show any interested prospects how marketable the Taney Motorsports' driver was. Which was essential, because Will's lackluster racing wasn't about to open wallets.

Despite what she chose to see as Taney's joke about the fees, Sandra was convinced that when they found a new sponsor, Taney would agree to her proposal to substantially increase his team's P.R. budget, both for Will and for his NASCAR Nationwide Series driver, who currently received only a tiny slice of the P.R. pie. And if Taney spent more, and if Will's brother, Bart, another client of Sandra's, also found a new sponsor, then there was a chance she'd make those loan repayments, save her business from going under, be able to pay for her parents' care…

Way too many ifs for a sound financial strategy. But it was all she had.

Sandra's cell phone rang, and she pounced on it. "Will?"

"Sandra, it's Anton Zakursky," said an older male voice.

"Dr. Zakursky." The other major worry in her life, one she simply didn't have time for now. She darted a glance at the clock. "You're calling early."

"I wanted to make sure you don't miss another appointment. We're okay for eleven today?"

Sandra closed her eyes. "Uh, I'm so sorry, I already forgot…and I'm in Chicago."

There was a long, disappointed silence from the doctor.

"Can I make another appointment for next week?" she asked. Dr. Zakursky told her to contact his receptionist during office hours, then said goodbye.

Sandra glared at the phone, willed Will to call.

"Are you sick?" Taney asked.

"Not at all." Just paranoid. Probably.

His hazel eyes flicked over her. "Do you work out?"

Sandra's hands went involuntarily, protectively, to her hips. "I beg your pardon?" Beneath her fingers she felt little pads of flesh where, ten years ago, there'd been angles and hollows.

The progress of his eyes had slowed and now his inspection lingered as it moved up to her face. "You look as if you do."

Or did he mean she looked as if she needed to?

Sandra stiffened. "I hardly think that's your business."

The gleam in those eyes might have been amusement. "You asked about the sponsor hunt. Her Fitness has decided to sponsor Will."

Just like that, a chunk of Sandra's worries evaporated.

"Taney, that's fantastic." Her Fitness was a national chain of women's gyms—which explained Taney's sudden interest in Sandra's workout regime. "I don't use their gyms, but they have a great reputation." Her mind raced ahead to the business implications. "When can we make an announcement? I need to work out some dates for a press conference. If only I'd known you were talking to them, I—"

Taney held up a large hand. "Whoa. The lawyers are making alterations to the contract this morning—we'll sign this afternoon. The company's based here in Chicago." He leaned back, propped one foot on the other knee and folded his arms in justifiable self-satisfaction. "You could probably meet with their marketing people at the end of today."

"Absolutely." She sagged onto the chair opposite his couch, and grinned at him. This news might not have her laughing all the way to the bank, but she deemed a chuckle quite permissible.

In response, his mouth curved in a slow smile—more unpracticed than grudging—that lightened his hazel eyes.

It struck Sandra there was something secretive about that smile. "There's more, isn't there? Something you're not telling me."

Immediately, his mouth firmed and he abandoned his laconic position for both-feet-on-the-floor assertiveness. He looked down his patrician nose at her. Although Taney was a self-made man, she'd heard his family was old money from back east—when he looked like this, she believed it.

"If there's anything you need to know, I'll be sure and tell you," he said.

If Taney played his cards any closer to his chest, he'd be performing open-heart surgery. Sandra clamped her hands on her knees and counted to five.

"Quit treating me as if I'm the enemy." Darn, she should have gone for ten—the asperity she'd been determined to tone down made an appearance. Gideon Taney always brought out the worst in her, which was frustrating, given that being tactful was a big part of her job and she didn't normally have a problem with it. She tried again, managed to say patiently, "Taney, you spend twenty thousand dollars a month with Motor Media Group, and you—"

"You think it's too much?" he deadpanned.

"Actually, it's too little," she retorted, before she remembered she wasn't going to mention that until after today's show. She leaned back into the cushions, crossed her ankles. "Was Her Fitness pleased that Will's on the *Olivia Winton Show?*"

He shrugged. "Nobody handed me a bouquet."

TANEY STIFLED A GROAN when Sandra's blue eyes lit up like fireflies.

"Really?" she said happily. "They were that impressed?"

He grunted something noncommittal; her smile widened. Dammit, she always knew when he was bluffing. But observing the curve of her lips and the gleam in her blue eyes, which were set in an oval face framed by waves of deep red hair, was safer than noticing the length of her legs in her above-the-knee skirt, or the curviness of her figure. As always, Taney put those images out of his mind, and prepared to spar with her. Because the next words out of her mouth would be a demand for more money.

"It was a huge amount of work getting Will onto this show," she said, an approach Taney deemed marginally more subtle than usual. "Most of my personal time that went into it wasn't covered by our fee. That's not counting the hours spent dealing with the fallout from Will's family problems. I didn't begrudge you those hours—" she spread her hands generously "—because I know how important it is to find a new sponsor. But if you want more opportunities like this…"

Why did she always push so hard? Taney was all in favor of enthusiasm and persistence. But he'd never met anyone so determined to make a go of her business—and so determined to use his money to do it. He knew Sandra must have borrowed a large sum to buy out her former partner in Motor Media Group. But she was a single woman with no ties, and the company must have a strong cash flow—she should be financially secure. Which made her shameless attempts to finagle more money from Taney Motorsports nothing more than naked ambition.

He admired her for it.

But if she was determined, he was more determined. No matter that she would do a good job with more money, or that the Olivia Winton interview had helped reassure Her Fitness that Will Branch's youthful good looks would attract mainstream media coverage. Taney had his own agenda, one he didn't plan to share with Sandra.

"I have no intention of increasing the team's P.R. spend." It came out harshly, but anything less would have opened the way to more badgering.

Something hot and pure—shock, maybe, or anger—flashed across her face. Instantly it cooled to disapproval.

No surprise there. Taney didn't have much involvement with Sandra; he left the day-to-day running of Taney Motorsports to his team manager, Jason Kemp. But every time he met with her, no matter that she was always polite, that undercurrent of disapprobation washed up against him. It bugged the heck out of him.

Without a hint of pride he could say he was one of the most respected team owners in NASCAR—he got along with everyone and he ran a tight ship. But on some mysterious Sandra-scale, he fell short.

"You might get a better feel for the value of your P.R. investment," Sandra said, her mouth tight, as if she was holding in a bunch of words that badly wanted to break out, "if you spent more time with the team."

A short, charged silence.

Then her stomach growled. The porcelain skin of her face colored up, but though she stood and rubbed a vigorous fist over her middle, she held Taney's gaze.

"I'm here today, aren't I?" he said. Of course, that was because the show coincided with the Her Fitness meeting, and had nothing to do with Sandra's e-mail—and two phone messages—demanding he come to Chicago to support Will. As if Will was a kid who needed someone to hold his hand.

The thought of his driver, whose resounding mediocrity made a late-April sponsor hunt more challenging than Taney needed it to be, prompted him to steamroller over whatever point she was trying to make. "Will's the one you should be concerned about right now." He glanced up at the TV screen on the wall. Olivia was interviewing her first guest, a self-help guru whose book was number one on all the bestseller lists.

TANEY WAS RIGHT, Sandra admitted to herself. But not to him—he already had way too much rocklike immovability about him for her to let him think he knew best. But

18   FULLY ENGAGED

Will's absence was starting to worry her. She couldn't have forgotten to give him some vital detail, such as the time he was due at the studio, could she? It wouldn't be the first thing she'd forgotten recently, just ask Dr. Zakursky. If this was her fault; if she'd botched this…

Suddenly nauseous, she stood, turned on her heel so she wouldn't have to face Taney, and tried Will's cell phone. Still switched off. She left him another message, then dialed the hotel, but got no answer from his room. He was definitely in Chicago, she'd flown in from Charlotte with him and his twin brother, Bart—another NASCAR Sprint Cup Series driver—yesterday. Maybe Bart had led Will astray. She tried Bart's room and there was no reply there, either.

"Blasted Brat Pack," she muttered.

"Excuse me?" Taney said.

She grimaced. "It's my private name for Will and Bart. They're okay on their own, but when you put the two of them together…" She tucked her phone back into the pocket of her pale gray silk-linen-blend suit jacket. "Though I'm sure everything's fine," she added meaninglessly. Heated by her growing alarm, she took her jacket off and dropped it over the back of the chair she'd vacated.

Once again, Taney's eyes traveled over her—all that talk about women's fitness must have gone to his head. Sandra knew better than to react by hunching her shoulders or folding her arms, which women as well-endowed as she was often felt obliged to do. The silky white blouse that draped in a *V* across her front would have been entirely modest on a smaller woman. On Sandra, it did show a little cleavage, but nothing that could be called flagrant.

A surge of sudden, restless energy seemed to propel Taney to his feet. "I'll go look for Will," he said gruffly.

He left the room, and right away oxygen flooded in, freeing Sandra to breathe deeply, setting her temples buzzing.

Taney couldn't have meant what he said about not increasing her budget, could he? It didn't make sense, with a new sponsor coming on board. Despite his unwillingness to talk, Sandra was sure Her Fitness had been impressed by the *Olivia Winton Show* deal. Taney was just playing hardball, she told herself. She rubbed the goose bumps on her arms.

The door opened, and Sandra braced herself for another round with Taney. But it was the young production assistant who'd promised to bring Will in when he arrived. She was alone.

"Uh, Sandra, there's no sign of Will," she said. "We do have another guest lined up if he's a no-show…?" Her voice tailed up in a question.

"He's almost here, my colleague went to fetch him." Sandra closed her eyes and prayed for Will's arrival.

"Okay," the girl said hesitantly, still willing, if barely, to rely on Sandra's self-proclaimed stellar record for delivering on her promises.

When she left, Sandra checked her watch—ten minutes until showtime. She pulled out her cell and jabbed at it to redial Will.

WILL FINALLY SAUNTERED in to the greenroom with just five minutes to spare before his segment started—and without Taney.

Sandra's first instinct, to plant a grateful kiss on him, was swiftly superseded by a wave of anger. "Where the heck have you been?"

As he headed for the coffeepot, he slanted her the lazy smile that charmed female fans, but which Sandra always felt indicated a lack of backbone. "Keep your hair on, Sandy. I'm here now."

Uh-oh. No one called her Sandy. *No one.* Not if they valued their health. Not unless they were out of their senses. Or unless they were…

Sandra registered Will's unnatural rigidity, the faint trembling of his hand as he poured a cup of coffee. The awful truth hit her. "You're drunk!"

"I am not." Will managed to sound outraged, even as he abandoned the coffee and sank onto the couch with exaggerated care. "I was drunk last night," he admitted. "Okay, maybe early this morning. But my only problem now is a slight headache."

Sandra didn't waste time asking how he could have been so stupid. Will Branch was immature and spoiled—that was a given. Later, she would tear him apart and donate his carcass to the North Carolina Zoo. Right now, she had four minutes to decide what to do with him.

She paced in front of the couch, pinching the bridge of her nose to aid clarity of thought. "Couldn't you have walked under a bus? Internal injuries would be much easier to explain."

"That's not nice." He switched to his hurt, puppy-dog look. Sandra was unmoved. Even if Will wasn't several years younger than she was, she wouldn't be interested in him. You could tell just by looking at him that he was irresponsible.

Funny how that showed in a man's face, just the way Taney's unquestionable strength of character—which, admittedly, she more often called pigheadedness—showed in his.

"Plus, you'd get a lot of sympathetic media coverage if you were in the hospital," she said. "Whereas now, you won't get any."

It took a second for her words to sink in. Then Will jumped to his feet, wincing with the suddenness of the movement. "You can't take me off the show," he protested. "Sandra, I'm not drunk, I swear. I'm sorry I went out last night, it was a dumb thing to do. A pal of Bart's was having a party—"

She might have known his twin had something to do with it, Sandra fumed, as he rambled through his explanation.

"I won't let you down," Will beseeched her. "I know how hard you've worked to get this interview set up and I'm not going to blow it."

At least someone appreciated her efforts. Will's face was more serious than she'd seen before. No trace of that juvenile arrogance, just the intent to do his best.

Could she let him go on the show?

For a second, Sandra wished Taney was here—he had a way of cutting to the heart of the matter that let him make quick but well-considered decisions.

Then she remembered she didn't usually agree with those decisions.

Taney would tell her there was no way his driver would go on air if he wasn't a hundred percent sober.

Taney didn't have a business that couldn't pay its bills. He didn't have the family responsibilities that weighed so heavily on Sandra they threatened to drive her into the ground.

"Please, Sandra," Will said, quietly, soberly.

She juggled her options. If Will had been falling-down, spit-in-your-eye drunk, she'd have pulled him off the show that instant. No matter that the consequences would have been horrendous—her hard-won reputation for reliability would be lost, she would never again get a client on to this or any other big TV show and Taney would probably fire her for not managing her client better.

She eyed Will. He was on that cusp of drunkenness where you had to look pretty hard to see it, and he was heading toward sobriety. If he hadn't called her *Sandy,* she realized, she wouldn't have noticed his condition. She'd have put his shaking hands down to nerves, and his slow gait likely wouldn't have registered.

"I promise you, the last drink I had was about three this morning."

No wonder he looked tired. But tired wasn't the same as drunk. A glance at her watch gave an unpleasant reminder of how little time they had. Two minutes. *Tick-tick.*

She grabbed the coffee he'd poured, shoveled sugar into it, then rammed the cup into his hands. "Drink this." And when he just stood there, looking at it, she ordered, "Now!"

He chugged it, made a face at the sweetness, but kept drinking.

Ideally, Sandra should have weighed the risks of putting Will on the show without considering the impact on her own future. But objectivity was impossible.

One minute to go.

Will could sometimes be a little raucous, but when he'd had a couple of drinks he tended to mellow out—and get funnier, more charming. Those qualities would serve him well in his interview with Olivia.

"Whaddya say, Sandra, do I go on?" Will shoved a hand through the curly blond hair that drove girls crazy.

"You're eye candy," Sandra said with a sudden sense of revelation.

He blinked. "Uh, sure."

"This is a breakfast show, a chat show, not a hard-hitting news show."

"That's right," he encouraged her.

She couldn't bear to think of her reputation slipping away, and all that would follow down the track.

Half a minute.

On days like this Sandra wanted to be a little girl again, curled up on her mama's lap. But she was too big to go on anyone's lap, and the buck stopped with her for everything, including her parents.

The door opened. The production assistant again. "I heard you were here," she cooed at Will, eyelashes fluttering. "We're in the commercial break right before your segment. I need to take you out there now, there's a makeup girl waiting—she'll do what she can."

Will shot a pleading glance at Sandra.

She let out a breath. "You're on."

"Yes!" He punched the air, and this time the movement didn't seem to affect his headache. See, he was better already.

"Thanks, Sandra." He hurried out behind the assistant, his walk steady, his eyes on the woman's bottom in a way that suggested he was his normal self.

Confidence swelled inside Sandra, displacing the anxiety. Anxiety, she now realized, brought on by Gideon Taney's implicit disapproval and his refusal to reconsider the budget. She'd let him rob her of her assurance.

Thank goodness she'd found it again in time to make her decision—undoubtedly different from the one Taney would have made, but she was happy with it.

What was the worst that could happen?

CHAPTER TWO

SANDRA SLIPPED into a seat at the back of the studio just as Olivia Winton announced that the show's next guest was "rising NASCAR star Will Branch"—a phrase taken directly from the briefing materials Sandra had supplied, rather than based on Will's performance on the track.

The studio audience—ninety-five percent female, as Sandra had expected—hollered and whooped as Will walked on stage. She congratulated herself on reading the situation correctly: these women would be more interested in his hot body than anything he said. Sandra cast a dispassionate eye over Will. None of last night's excesses showed in his graceful bearing, his warm smile and his firm clasp of Olivia's hand, which was followed by a kiss—apparently spontaneous, but in fact coached by Sandra—on the host's cheek. The audience cheered the kiss.

Sandra let her shoulders sag. *It's going to be fine.*

"Our boy's quite a showman." The words, spoken softly in her ear, made her jump. She didn't need to look around to identify the speaker whose warm breath sent a shiver across her neck.

"You think?" she said nervously. Taney was the only other person observant enough to notice Will's inebriation.

She pulled herself together, before her jitters made him suspicious. "This audience must be right in Her Fitness's target market. They love him."

Will bowed to the still-applauding crowd. Okay, that was a little over-the-top, but no one objected, and a few wolf whistles rose above the noise of the clapping.

Sandra chanced a sidelong glance at Taney, saw him nod in agreement.

"Her Fitness did have doubts as to whether a 'second-rate,' as they put it, driver like Will would have sufficient mass market appeal," he admitted.

When she didn't say anything, he nudged her arm. "Aren't you going to jump on me with a hefty new contract to sign?"

The superserious Gideon Taney was teasing her—she chalked it up to one more moment of weirdness in this crazy day. He was right, that was exactly what she should do. But she'd lost the stomach for a fight. All she wanted was for this interview to be over. She forced a weak smile at Taney.

On stage, Will looked calm and confident—and sober—as he settled on the studio's couch.

"Will Branch, welcome to the show. You've got to be the best-looking guest we've had in a long time—and I'm including those romance novel cover models," Olivia said generously.

Will smiled at her, his dimples deepening. Somewhere in the audience, Sandra heard a woman sigh. "Thanks, Olivia, you're looking great yourself." He leaned forward and picked up the glass of water on the table in front of him. *Dehydrated,* Sandra thought.

Something about Taney—an increased alertness?—

made her turn to him. His eyes were on Will. He said, "Something's up."

What? What was up? Sandra's head swiveled back toward the stage. What had Taney seen?

"He's doing okay," she said, reassuring herself as much as him.

Olivia asked Will a couple of easy questions about the life of a NASCAR Sprint Cup Series driver. He handled them perfectly.

"Will, you've had more headlines than you wanted recently, and they haven't been about your racing," Olivia said, her voice a blend of sympathy and curiosity.

"She's going to ask about Hilton," Taney hissed.

A couple of months earlier, Hilton Branch, Will's father, had absconded with millions of dollars from the bank of which he was president. He was still at large, and the case was garnering a ton of media attention.

The bank had been Will's and Bart's primary sponsor. The management's natural reaction to the theft—pulling the plug on both drivers—and the media storm it had created were the cause of Sandra's current woes.

"The producer said they couldn't ignore it," Sandra murmured. "But they've agreed to tackle it sympathetically and get the topic out of the way early."

It had been a fair compromise—Olivia Winton would look stupid if she ignored that Will's father was America's most-wanted white-collar criminal. The approach they'd agreed upon would sustain her credibility and at the same time emphasize Will's admirable loyalty to his family. And, hopefully, engage the audience's sympathies.

In an aside to the audience, Olivia gave a brief summary

of Hilton Branch's alleged crime. "What are your feelings about what your father did?" she asked Will.

This was where Will would say he'd hoped his father was innocent, but right now it didn't look that way. That although he was angry, he loved his dad and wanted to hear the truth directly from him. Will took a swallow from the glass of water he held.

In his left hand.

In a burst of clarity, the morning's events rewound in Sandra's head, superfast, then coalesced to form an entirely different picture.

She cursed, a word she'd never said before in her life. One that would have been covered by a loud bleep if she'd been up on stage.

"Are you okay?" Taney's fingers circled her wrist and clamped tight. He'd never touched her before, beyond a handshake. She longed, for the briefest moment, to lean in to him.

"Sandra, what's the matter?"

Her mouth moved, but her brain was still working through the implications of her discovery, and no words came out. She tried again, remembered to keep it to a whisper. "That's not Will up there. It's Bart."

In the absence of an immediate answer from Will, Olivia was expanding on her question. Words like *fraud* and *shame* floated off the stage.

Taney shook Sandra's wrist. "Are you sure?"

"Bart's left-handed, Will's right."

He looked up at the stage, registered the water glass. "Why the— No, we'll figure that out later. Just tell me, do we have a problem?"

Ha ha ha! Manic laughter rose in Sandra's head. Ten

out of ten to Taney for recognizing her incipient hysteria. He tugged her out of her seat and hurried her back to the greenroom, where he pushed her none too gently onto the couch.

"Explain," he ordered.

On the TV above them, Olivia had run out of things to say, and was waiting for Will to speak, concerned sympathy on her face. Sandra could feel Bart's tension from here. How could she have been so stupid as to allow him to go on stage? She swallowed. "Will—Bart—is drunk."

Taney gaped. Then his jaw set in a firm line and he said grimly, "You knew he was drunk and you let him go out there?"

"Inebriated." She regretted her stark first choice of words. "Tipsy, really."

On screen, Bart answered the question. He followed the script Sandra had agreed to with Will, more or less, and he was still smiling. But there was an edge to it. It was one thing for the Branches to condemn their father within the family— talking about it on TV was another matter altogether. Bart hadn't had time to prepare mentally for public disclosure.

Sandra drew a deep breath. "We do have a problem," she confessed. "When Will gets drunk, he gets funnier." The memory of last year's client Christmas party played vividly in her head. "When Bart gets drunk, he gets…louder."

Taney's dark eyebrows knit together.

"More aggressive," Sandra said miserably, remembering how she'd stepped in to break up a brawl and almost been decked before Bart realized who she was.

On the TV screen, Olivia said, "Did you know your father was stealing from the bank?"

Will was supposed to deny all knowledge, then express regret for anyone who'd been hurt by the missing money, whether it was his dad's fault or not. Because, to the rest of the world, his father should be innocent until proven guilty.

Bart's face darkened.

"Did your mother know?" Olivia asked.

"Uh-oh," Sandra murmured.

"Leave my mother out of this," Bart said loudly. "Since this happened, the media have been a pack of vultures who can't wait to feed on my family's misery. You're a bunch of—" A series of bleeps overrode his words, all except the last one, which happened to be *morons*. The camera panned to the shocked studio audience.

Olivia's eyebrows shot up. She looked furious, understandably, given Bart's comment was clearly intended to include her. "Has your father been in touch with you or your family?"

"How can he, when our phones are probably tapped?" Bart demanded rudely.

The camera zoomed in on Olivia, her face now a tight mask. "Your father has brought shame on your family and damaged your racing career—"

She was going beyond the questions Sandra had agreed to with the producer, and who could blame her?

"Hey!" Bart leapt to his feet. "No one got hurt except a bunch of fat-cat bankers caught out with egg on their faces." He was yelling now. "We have enough trouble with the cops hounding us. I don't need some overweight bimbo TV host—" the audience gasped, as Olivia Winton's weight was a notoriously sensitive subject "—sticking her big nose into my family's problems."

Olivia straightened her spine and fixed Bart with an icily regal glare that reminded everyone she was the queen of talk. "Given the Branch family is so keen on its privacy, the recent intimate revelations by Hilton Branch's longtime mistress must have been somewhat…irritating?"

Sandra whimpered. Taney groaned.

From what should have been rock-bottom, the interview went downhill fast. Bart and Olivia launched into a shouting match that enthralled the audience and would undoubtedly make the network news tonight. It lasted until Bart stormed offstage. The audience gave Olivia a standing ovation for facing down a guest who was such a jerk.

In the greenroom, Sandra said, "Taney, I'm sorry—"

His scowl slammed into her apology, knocking the wind out of it.

"Stay right where you are," he snapped.

THE PLAN HAD BEEN for drinks and snacks to be served in the greenroom after the show, so Will and Olivia could chat less formally.

Instead, Olivia disappeared to wherever celebrity show hosts went when they were too mad to speak. Taney went out to find Bart and hauled him into the room.

"You idiot." He didn't hold back, delivering an articulate assessment of Bart's personality as he shoved him down onto the couch next to Sandra. Sandra got up—if she stayed this close, she'd slug him.

Bart was still breathing heavily, his face red. "Did you hear what that witch was saying about my family?"

"Get over it," Sandra snapped. "Where is Will?"

Bart flinched at the realization he'd been found out. "He's sick."

"Hung over?" Taney asked.

Bart shook his head. "He came with me to the party last night, but he didn't drink. He didn't want to risk it ahead of the show. But he woke up this morning with the worst case of food poisoning you ever saw. I left him on the can and I'll bet he's still there."

Sandra pushed aside the unpleasant image. "Why didn't you tell me?"

"Will was desperate not to miss out on the show—he knows he'll never get a chance like this again. I said I'd come instead." It wasn't the first time the twins had pulled a switcheroo—they were both practical jokers. "It's never got us into trouble before," Bart said defensively.

"I ought to take you two apart and sell you as shark bait," Taney snarled. It was so close to Sandra's earlier intention to turn Will into zoo-food that she started.

"I only had a few drinks." Bart buried his face in his hands, and Sandra noticed he was shaking. It might be true that he hadn't drunk much—she should have realized that the late night and early start would have compounded the effect of the alcohol.

"A few too many," Taney corrected.

"Obviously, if I'd known I was going to be on TV with that fat cow—"

"Enough," Taney roared.

Bart fell silent. And once again, Sandra's stomach picked a prime moment to grumble.

Taney rounded on her. "Will you stop doing that?"

"Not 'til I have my breakfast," she retorted. "How about *you* stop all this prowling and roaring?" He reminded her of an enraged lion. "You might find it satisfying, but it's not getting us anywhere. We've screwed up—"

"You screwed up," Taney corrected.

"And now *we* need to figure out what to do."

He looked as if he had some ideas that revolved around staking her to a racetrack and letting the entire fleet of NASCAR Sprint Cup Series cars drive over her. But before he could share them, his cell phone rang.

TANEY HAD BY NO MEANS finished giving Sandra a piece of his mind—hell, he hadn't even started—so although reflex had him pulling his phone out of his pocket, his thumb went straight for the off button. Then he saw the number.

Damn. He was tempted to go ahead and switch the thing off. But from the moment Bart had lost control in his interview, Taney had known this call was coming. If any window existed for damage limitation, it was now.

"Mary, I guess you saw the show."

"Forget it." Mary Kelly, the hard-nosed, sharp-minded CEO of Her Fitness didn't waste time. "If you think we'd pay money to have that loose cannon represent us…if you think women want to go to a gym whose spokesman insulted Olivia Winton—one of the most revered women in America—about her weight, you're nuts."

Explaining that Will and Bart had swapped places would hardly make Will seem more reliable. "Today wasn't the best timing for the show." Not exactly a compelling response. "Will's been under a lot of pressure."

"Which brings me to my next point," Mary Kelly fumed. "You said he would keep quiet about his father."

There was nothing Taney could say to placate her. He told her he'd call her next week, but they both knew she wouldn't change her mind.

FROM THE FIRM SET of Taney's jaw and the hard look he sent her as he ended the call, Sandra figured Her Fitness had pulled out of the deal. Visions of paying her loans evaporated.

"You just lost your brother a new sponsor," Taney said to Bart.

Bart looked momentarily guilty, but then he said sulkily, "You'll find someone else." He eyed Sandra, and the deep *V* of her blouse. Insolently, he said, "Just take Sandra with you and have her flash those killer—"

Taney grabbed him by the collar and twisted, hauling him off the sofa. "Watch your mouth," he growled.

Taney was defending her? So soon after wanting to stake her to a racetrack? Guilt flip-flopped in Sandra's stomach—either that, or she was so hungry her stomach was eating itself.

"I can look after myself," she said to Taney. Because she didn't deserve his defense. Not when it was her fault they'd lost Her Fitness.

He let Bart go. The younger man glowered as he tugged the neck of his shirt back into place.

"Any more comments like that," she told Bart, "and you'll be trying to convince a hundred reporters that the official press release announcing your impotence was a hoax."

Bart recoiled. The sound from Taney might have been a laugh, but when Sandra glanced at him, he still looked mad, with both her and Bart.

"Well?" she demanded.

"Sorry," Bart mumbled.

"We're not going to fix this here," Taney said. "Bart, drag your brother out of bed, take him back to Charlotte.

Did you come on the team plane?" Bart nodded. "Tell him I want to see him tomorrow, I don't care how sick he is.

"You—" he turned to Sandra, and his mouth was so uncompromising she wondered how she could have imagined that laugh "—get to come with me. We need to talk."

When she'd woken this morning, she'd let her imagination wander ahead to this part of the day. Funnily enough, her mental picture had included Taney saying, "We need to talk." Followed by him signing a check.

Sandra hadn't graduated summa cum laude from Duke without the brains to figure out there would be no check today.

She gulped, but it wasn't enough to swallow the bitter truth.

Taney was about to fire her.

CHAPTER THREE

IF TANEY HAD NEEDED a reminder that his heart was no longer in NASCAR, this was it.

As they took off from O'Hare in his private jet, he wasn't worrying about what Bart's stunt and the continued lack of a sponsor would do to team morale, or even about whether they could afford to race through to the Chase for the NASCAR Sprint Cup.

All he could think about was how Sandra's appalling lapse of judgment would affect his personal plans.

Although he'd schooled his face into its usual distant impassivity, he was so mad he could shake her. Which he didn't consider inappropriate conduct, because she was tall enough and tough enough to look after herself.

Though to make it a fair fight, she'd probably have to slip out of those gray high-heeled shoes with the pink bow at the toes, so she'd be steadier on her feet. Taney's ill-disciplined gaze dropped to her slim ankles.

And she hadn't exactly looked tough when her blue eyes had gone wide and anxious, and her face pale, when she'd realized it was Bart up there on stage.

He allowed his gaze to wander past her, sitting in the black leather upholstered seat next to his in the center of the airplane, as if he wasn't really seeing her. It was a

useful skill he'd acquired back when he'd started All
Sports, the sporting goods company that was now one of
the largest chains in the country. The ability to look around
with apparent vacancy, all the while taking in every detail
of the sales graphs on a rival's office wall, was of immea-
surable value.

Not that Sandra was a rival, as she'd pointed out earlier.
They were on the same side…and if this had been a basketball game, Taney would have chosen her for his team. He
guessed she could be as much as six feet tall. She was curvy,
but not overweight, and with that red hair complementing her
creamy complexion, very striking. If she couldn't play ball,
she'd do a damned good job of distracting the competition.

Taney yanked his thoughts back. This wasn't a game,
this was business, and Sandra was responsible for a royal
screwup. It was inexcusable.

He almost wished she would let rip with some kind of
excuse, some argument that would justify him ripping into
her in return. But she'd avoided his eyes since they got on
the plane. Her long lashes shielded her thoughts, but the
droop of her full lips hinted at a vulnerability that made it
hard for him to yell.

She'd probably guessed his intention. A twinge of guilt
pinched him, but he shook it off. She'd find another client,
that wasn't his problem. She deserved this, dammit.

But he couldn't say what had to be said if she wouldn't
look at him.

He reached into his jacket pocket, pulled out the Krispy
Kreme bag he'd all but forgotten.

"Here." He pushed it into the nest made by the fingers
she'd laced in her lap.

Sandra jumped, as though she'd forgotten he was there.

Which annoyed Taney, when he was so aware of her. "What's this?" Her voice came out quiet, and she cleared her throat.

"What it looks like—breakfast. I picked it up when I went out to find Will before the show." *Before you messed up my plans.* "Your stomach was so loud I thought it might scare the kids in the audience."

She colored—the curse of that fair complexion, he assumed—but returned feistily, "Your yelling would have scared them more—they probably heard you all the way from the greenroom." She opened the bag and sniffed the contents. Her tongue came out and licked her lips. Taney shifted in his seat. "Mmm, apple cinnamon," she murmured. She crumpled the bag closed and said without much resolution, "I shouldn't. The carbs…"

"Eat," Taney ordered. "I want to talk to you and you're going to need your strength."

Her head jerked around, and for a moment she looked downright scared, which irked Taney—as if he was some kind of monster!

She pulled the donut from the bag and bit into it, leaving a trail of powdered cinnamon on her lips. "Thank you, this was very thoughtful of you."

Okay, he wasn't a monster, but he didn't want Sandra getting any fanciful ideas about him being a soft touch.

"Is there anything else you'd like to say about this morning?" He hardened his voice. He would hear her out, but then he'd do what he had to.

His tone had the effect of wiping away that fragility he'd seen. Sandra straightened in her seat, took her time finishing a mouthful. Then she looked him square in the eye. "What would you have done, if you were me?"

The question took him by surprise, but he didn't hesitate. "If I'd guessed Will was drunk, I'd never have put him on TV."

"Despite the fact you'd put everything into setting up that show? Despite knowing that in one day you'd blow the reputation it took years to earn for delivering on your promises?"

He let the raise of an eyebrow point out that today's fiasco could do as much damage to her reputation as pulling Will from the show might have. She bit her lip, but didn't look away.

"As much or more time and effort goes into every NASCAR Sprint Cup Series race," Taney said, "but I wouldn't let my driver get into a race car drunk."

She caught her breath. "It would have been all right if it was Will," she said, more to herself than him. "The problem was Bart."

He couldn't believe she still thought there'd been anything smart about her decision. "You don't even know your client well enough to recognize him."

"They're identical," she snapped. "If they'd been side by side I might have been able to—"

"Sandra—" he'd like to do this more graciously, but if she couldn't see reason "—you're fired."

He felt like a certain reality TV show host, only with way better hair. And, it seemed, less authority. Sandra didn't react the way people did on the show—there was no stunned acceptance of her fate.

She let out a little hiss, then, as if she couldn't bear to be so close to him, she unclipped her seat belt and stood, brushing the empty donut bag to the floor. She took a couple of steps backward. "You can fire me if you want—"

"I just did." See, this was the trouble with her, she never understood who was boss. He didn't need her permission to fire her.

"But you need to admit that at least half the blame is yours," she continued.

Outrage almost winded Taney. "Did anyone tell you it's unprofessional to blame others for your mistakes?"

"No." She sat in the seat on the other side of the coffee table, facing him. "But I have a feeling you're about to give me a textbook example."

Taney folded his arms, stared her down. "I'm not the one who let a drunk race car driver, impersonating her client go on a major TV show." It had all the tacky splendor of a tabloid headline, and if anyone else ever found out the truth about today, that's exactly where the story would end up.

She came back, blue eyes blazing, her anger shrinking the physical distance between them to nothing. "No, you're not," she raged. "You're the arrogant, close-mouthed jerk who would rather let his whole team suffer an agony of indecision than share details of what he's doing to save it. You're the man who runs his race team like a feudal absentee dictator, never bothering to show up unless it's to punish us for our incompetence. You're the—"

"You've said enough," Taney roared, and some small part of him was aware this was what he'd wanted all along, an argument with someone who wasn't so intimidated that he had to worry about wounding her, someone who gave back as good as she got. He'd been resentful and annoyed for so long—not with her, not even with the team, but with life—but he was so used to keeping his distance from people that he never got the chance to vent.

"Then you have the nerve to fire me—" to his maddened delight, she continued as if he hadn't spoken "—when if you'd shown one *scrap* of interest in Will Branch's performance this season, he'd never have gone out to a party last night, never have ended up with food poisoning."

"I've made the rules about driver behavior quite clear," he thundered.

"Ooh, the rules," she said with mock awe. "You mean those decrees that come down from on high, relayed through your lackey Kemp because you can't be bothered showing up at the team headquarters more than once a month?"

Actually, it had been once every couple of months recently, but Taney wasn't about to admit that. "What you may not understand, Ms. Jacobs," he said icily, "given your lack of experience in running multimillion-dollar enterprises, is the art of delegation."

"I *understand* that you washed your hands of this team months ago," she retorted. "If you think you'll get the best out of your people when it's obvious you've lost interest, then you don't know the first thing about leadership."

"What the—? I'm a born leader, dammit, and if you want proof, take a look at my business. Put it alongside yours, and tell me who's the leader here." Blood rushed to Taney's temples; his heart thudded hard and fast. No one challenged him like this, not in years. He hadn't felt this exhilarated since those early days with the team, when every start, every finish in a NASCAR race, had been a heart-stopping battle.

He glared at Sandra, but she didn't give an inch. Her bosom heaved in a way that drew his attention, reminded him of her incredible figure. Taney clamped a hand to his brow. This was crazy, she was insulting him and he was thinking about her body! Her breath came fast, like his, and suddenly the atmosphere seemed charged with a sensuous awareness that expanded and filled the airplane.

"Face it, Taney," she taunted, "you're not the right kind of guy to own a NASCAR team."

Anything sensuous vanished, leaving good old-fashioned anger in its place. "I won the Sprint Cup four years ago," he bellowed. "And I won the NASCAR Nationwide Series the year after."

"Notice how you said *you* won?" she asked, her voice quiet, in a way that Taney guessed was calculated to make him feel as if he was ranting. Which he was, but he was having a surprisingly good time and he wasn't ready to stop. "A good team owner would say *we* won." She squared her shoulders and looked him in the eye. "You're not a team player."

How had this got to be about him, when *she* was the one being fired?

"I *own* a team," Taney snarled. "Of course I'm a team player."

She shook her head, lifted her chin, as if she was trying to make herself as tall as he. He wondered where the top of her head would come to, if they were standing, if he took her shoes off. Of course, the way her eyes were spitting, she'd kick him if he tried.

"That you're firing me now, after one mistake, proves my point," she said.

Dammit, he was in the right, he knew he was, but she'd somehow seized the moral high ground. He had to forcibly remind himself he had nothing to prove. Unclipping his seat belt, he stood, strode to the bar fridge and pulled out a cola.

"Do you talk like this to Latimer?" he demanded. Richard Latimer was Bart's team owner. Of course, Latimer hadn't fired Sandra, so chances were she curbed her temper with him.

"Richard is not only a gentleman, he's a good communicator," Sandra said superciliously. "He's been open about his talks with EZ-Plus Software about Bart, and I've given him some input that will hopefully help him make a deal." Her foot tapped the carpet. "Are you going to offer me a drink?"

"You mean, like a *gentleman* would?"

She came over and grabbed her own soda. She looked him in the eye, unwavering, uncowed. He was taller than she was, but not as much as he was used to. He'd always used his size to his advantage; now he realized she did, too. This close, the heat between them was a palpable contrast to the ice-cold can he held.

"You, on the other hand—" she ignored his dig "—have consistently refused to say who you're talking to about Will. If I'd known about Her Fitness, I might have been able to help you convince them to sign sooner, before today's show. Will could have helped, too—for all his faults he does have a personality that appeals to sponsors."

"I'm not running the Will Branch fan club." He took an impatient swig of his cola. "This team is a business, and right now I have an urgent need to find a sponsor, which, believe me, is all about money, not personality."

"Good luck with that." Her tone suggested she wished him the opposite. "I'm very forgiving, so call me when you get tough questions about quantifying a sponsor's return on investment." She jabbed a finger in his direction. "Because that's not just about money—" *jab* "—it's about brand image and a whole lot of intangible stuff that happens to be my field of expertise." *Jab.* "Maybe, if you'd tapped in to that, this wouldn't be taking you so long."

Annoyed, Taney grabbed her finger mid-jab. "Enough with the Finger of Doom."

Her hand felt both strong and fine in his. He uncurled her fingers and their softness distracted him from the point he planned to make, namely that he'd had a great sponsor lined up until she'd blown it this morning.

He could also justifiably claim that he was running a megamillion-dollar sports equipment business at the same time as he was hunting for Will's sponsor, so it was no wonder his focus was diluted.

In fact, whichever way he looked at it, he was running out of time. If he didn't find a sponsor for Will soon, it would ruin all his plans.

Maybe he did need some help...and maybe he did need an injection of the kind of fire Sandra had brought out in him today. It had been so long since he'd felt any passion for the team; sponsors might detect that. And NASCAR wasn't a sport you invested in unless you were passionate.

SANDRA EXTRICATED her hand from Taney's with some difficulty. He wasn't consciously holding on to her—whereas she was hyperconscious that she was holding hands with a client—but his natural strength meant she had to employ some effort to gain her freedom.

She couldn't believe she'd lambasted him that way. But given he'd fired her, she had nothing to lose. And it had been a blessed relief to pour out some of the frustrations that had made life almost impossible the past year.

Over the rim of her soda can, she eyed Taney. Without his customary aloofness his eyes were more green than brown. His mouth, while still firm, seemed fuller, less set. That hint of softness turned him from someone she could objectively evaluate as a perfect specimen of manhood into a real man, whose maleness called to something female in her. Something entirely unrelated to her biological clock; this was more about a tug of attraction that—

"I'm willing to take you back on probation," he said abruptly.

She had her job back? Sandra severed the tug of attraction and filed it under Don't Go There. The realization that she might still have a chance of making her loan repayments this month swamped her, and she sat down before her knees gave way. "How long is the probation period?" She surprised herself with her calmness.

He threw her an exasperated look. "However long I say. As you so potently informed me, you know a lot about the return a sponsor will get. I want you focused on the sponsor hunt, as well as the media work." She opened her mouth, and he held up a hand. "Don't even think about asking me to expand the budget."

"Fine," Sandra said with a meekness born of relief that, not only did she still have the Taney Motorsports account, but they also must be nearly at Charlotte by now. Soon, she would get off this plane, get away from this man who provoked her to such unruly behavior and get on with her job. After the trauma of the day, it sounded enticingly simple. "I'll start work with Jason on Monday, and we'll figure out who else we can approach."

Now that Taney had set a course of action, he was back to his distant self. He reminded her of an oil tanker passing through a fleet of lesser craft, leaving them bobbing in his wake, impervious to the disturbance he'd created.

"Not Jason," Taney said coolly.

She waited.

"I can't afford any more foul-ups. You and I will work together." If his tone hadn't been so utterly disinterested, she'd have sworn his hazel eyes gleamed with devilment. "As a team."

TANEY'S IDEA of teamwork seemed to consist of regular phone calls to issue orders to Sandra. She was used to working in a more egalitarian style with Jason Kemp—if she was honest, she'd admit she was the one who gave Jason orders—so Taney's attitude had her hackles up more often than not. He made things worse by having no time to fit her in to his crammed schedule for a meeting.

At least she was spared the discomfort of seeing him again after their shouting match. But Taney's unavailability also made it impossible to narrow down the list of potential sponsors.

Sandra wondered how he had ever managed to inspire his team to capture the NASCAR Sprint Cup Series. Winning couldn't be done without a close-knit, full-on effort in which every person on the team—from the owner to the jackman—was acknowledged as having a vital role to play and respected for their contribution. The fact that Taney Motorsports had won both the NASCAR Sprint Cup Series championship as well as the NASCAR Nationwide Series championship gave her hope that Taney had the right stuff somewhere inside him.

Kylie Palmer, Will Branch's account manager, knocked on the open door of Sandra's office. "Did you want to see me?"

"Come in." Sandra glanced at her watch. It was eleven o'clock on Friday morning, and she hadn't visited her parents yet this week. The weekend was fully booked, so she'd have to make time this afternoon. Dad was never good in the afternoons, and she cursed her own slackness in not getting to him sooner. "I want to talk to you about Will," she told Kylie. "We have a major rescue job on our hands."

"The phone's been running hot all week," Kylie agreed. "I issued the statement we prepared, but I haven't let Will do any interviews yet."

"We need to get him into the media in a positive light, so we can counter the impact of his interview with Olivia," Sandra said. Only she, Taney and Kylie knew it was Bart, not Will, who'd made those offensive comments. Even the twins were sworn to secrecy. "I invited a couple of reliable reporters to join us for testing at Dallas this weekend. I know it's short notice, but I'd like your help."

"Maybe if you'd let me go to the studio," Kylie said carefully, "I'd have realized it wasn't Will. And we wouldn't be picking up the pieces now."

Sandra doubted that, but they would never know. She'd worked so hard on setting up the show, she hadn't wanted to hand over responsibility to Kylie. *I wanted Taney to give me the kudos.*

Talk about backfiring.

"I'd like to help, but I need to spend some time with Ryan this weekend." Kylie's ten-year-old son always came first in her life, and normally Sandra applauded that. But right now, she was inexplicably more conscious than usual of the things her life lacked—a husband, children, any kind of balance—and also resentful that she didn't have the luxury of staying in Charlotte this weekend to visit her parents. Her sympathy was worn to the bone.

"I'm afraid I will need you in Dallas for at least one day," she said pleasantly.

Kylie reluctantly agreed, and they discussed some angles that might get the reporters thinking positively about Will. Sandra turned the discussion to the next few races, only to have Kylie say, "Remember, I won't be at Talladega. Ryan has his soccer championship, and you promised me some vacation days."

Sandra groaned inwardly and pushed aside the longing that just this once someone would take something off her hands, then added the responsibility for Will at Talladega to the million other things on her list.

Her cell phone rang; it was Taney. She asked Kylie to wait while she took the call.

"It's time we met up," Taney said without preamble.

Her stomach gave the oddest lurch, but she said calmly, "I've been telling you that for several days."

"We'll have to do it this weekend."

"I can't, I'll be at the track in Texas."

"Sandra," Taney said, "the Texas race is *next* weekend."

"Taney," she said, "*your team* has a two-day testing session *this* weekend."

From his silence, she gathered she'd won this round. She took a moment to enjoy the victory, since she seemed to be losing every other battle.

"Testing in Dallas is perfect," he said, as if they'd arranged it just for his convenience. "I'll join you there. And I'm bringing a friend."

As if she cared about his social life. "Just so long as you're not too busy with your *friend* for us to plan our sponsor campaign," she said acidly.

Right away, he got assertive. "It's *my* sponsor campaign, so I'll decide how much time we need."

That's what he thought. Sandra planned to overwhelm him with the comprehensive list of potential sponsors and associated publicity ideas that she'd worked into the small hours the past few nights to create. Taney had said she couldn't ask for more money for publicity, so she wouldn't. She would just present him with ideas so irresistible that he'd beg her to implement them. At which point she would remind him regretfully there was no money left in the budget.

Ha!

She ended the call and got back to Kylie.

"I don't know if any of this will work." The younger woman contemplated her notes gloomily. "Will's image really took a pounding."

However subtle, it was censure Sandra didn't want to hear. As if she hadn't beaten herself up enough already.

"That's enough, Kylie." She pulled rank, Taney-style, and the sharpness in her voice cut off the other woman's words. "If you and I can't say anything positive, how on earth can we expect the media to? Your job depends on us keeping the Taney Motorsports account, so let's get out there and make sure the world knows Will Branch is a great guy anyone could be proud to sponsor."

Kylie's cheeks paled, but she said no more. As she left Sandra's office, she threw a look over her shoulder that might have been resentful, if not for a betraying quiver of anxiety. Sandra met it unflinchingly, and thanked Taney for the poker-face lessons.

If she was to survive the next few weeks, she would have to toughen up all around.

With a sigh, she plucked her keys off the desk and tugged her jacket from the back of her chair. She really didn't have time to visit Mom and Dad now, but her conscience wouldn't let her leave it.

I'll toughen up tomorrow.

CHAPTER FOUR

WILL'S CREW CHIEF, Seth Gallant, wanted to test some new setups on the No. 467 car, in the hope of damming the stream of Will's abysmal results. A large part of the problem appeared to be the communication between the driver and chief. Will's complaints that the car was too loose never got resolved to his satisfaction. Seth felt that by trying different configurations and getting feedback from Will every single time, they'd be able to make sure they were speaking the same language.

During a break while the team made some adjustments to the car, Sandra helped Kylie kick off the first of the media appointments—an interview with a TV crew from a local Dallas channel—then went to find Taney, who'd booked a suite for the day, which to her seemed excessive.

She realized en route to the suite that she'd forgotten one of her folders—she must have left it in the hauler.

"Blast." She headed back to the garage and tried to confine her feelings to exasperation. *Don't panic.* She had to get over this stupid fear that every forgetful moment meant she was about to succumb to the Alzheimer's disease that had claimed her father's mind far too early. But lately she'd been forgetting things more and more...and no matter how irrational, fear grabbed her by the gullet.

By the time she retrieved the folder—which was in her rental car, not in the hauler, making her memory lapse more severe than she'd thought—and scurried to the sponsor suite, Sandra was nearly fifteen minutes late. Taney's glance at his watch as she entered the room told her he'd noted her tardiness.

Keep your shirt on.

Bad thought. A vision of Taney minus his shirt assailed Sandra, bringing her to a halt right in front of him. Where had that come from? She'd always been aware of him but she'd never thought about him in a way that could be considered remotely sexual.

Apart from that repopulating-the-planet thing.

"Good morning, Sandra."

And the occasional internal squirm provoked by his deep voice, which some women might find sexy.

"Taney, nice to see you." Great, she was so frantic to restore her professional calm, she'd resorted to lying.

And he knew it, judging by the way one side of his mouth lifted, half-skeptical, half-amused. The Taney Motorsports polo shirt that clung to his chest and revealed powerful biceps made him look even bigger than usual. His black jeans emphasized the length of his legs—all up, he was a picture of power. It was a long time since she'd seen him in casual clothes—mainly because it was months since he'd attended a race—and she'd forgotten how they took away any veneer of restraint.

The April day was unseasonably warm, and Sandra's rush to get here had left her perspiring. She slipped out of her light wool jacket and slung it over a chair before she sat down at the table Taney indicated. He'd positioned the table immediately above the tiered seating that took up half the suite. Below them, through the massive window, Will's car flashed around the track alone. Sandra had the uncharitable thought that it was the only time he'd looked dominant this season.

"We don't have long." Taney checked his watch again.

He'd kept her waiting days for this meeting, and now he was making a big deal of her being a few minutes late. *I have a life, too, buster.* Or she planned to, one day. "Surely your girlfriend can survive without you for an hour," Sandra snapped.

He frowned. "What girlfriend?"

"The one you said you planned to bring today."

Taney looked at Sandra through hooded eyes. "I said *friend.*"

Oops.

"Interesting that you assumed I meant a girlfriend."

She read complacency in his tone, and knew what it meant: he thought she found him attractive. Since that fight last week, a simmering tension had underpinned their phone conversations. He obviously thought there was more to it than her annoyance with him. Taney didn't have the inflated ego of some of the drivers, who thought their uniforms made them irresistible to women. But he had a kind of arrogant acceptance about him that said he wasn't surprised she was attracted to him, and he was prepared to tolerate it.

Was she attracted? Beyond that pang of recognition she'd felt the other day? No, she didn't go for guys like Taney.

"From that tantrum you threw on the way back from Chicago," she said airily, "I thought you must be one of those insecure guys who needs a pretty girl to prop up his self-image."

Brilliant. She'd mentioned their fight, and put the blame on him. She braced herself for him to get mad.

Instead, he said suavely, "A natural assumption." Then he leaned back in his chair, hands behind his head, and stretched to his full, gorgeous, mouth-drying length, thereby proclaiming he had absolutely nothing to be insecure about.

His eyes lingered on the square neckline of Sandra's white T-shirt. *He definitely thinks I like him.* Sandra reined in her indignation and told herself to stop thinking like a fifteen-year-old.

"I invited my friend *Jack*—" Taney emphasized the male name "—to join me here at half past. His firm, Hoops and More, is interested in sponsoring Will."

Dallas-based Hoops And More was one of America's largest manufacturers of basketball equipment. But Taney couldn't expect Sandra to applaud, when once again he'd gone ahead without consulting her.

With slow, deliberate moves designed to counter her frustration, she unpacked her bag and set pens and folders out on the table. "Don't you think you should have told me you were in discussions with him, so I could be prepared for this meeting?"

"First up, I only arranged it after you told me yesterday we were coming to Dallas," Taney said. "Jack and I played basketball in college, and we still shoot a few hoops now and then. He's a buddy, there was no formal approach."

She'd heard from some of the guys on the race team that Taney had been a top college player in his day, who could have made the NBA, if he hadn't wanted to start his own business.

"More importantly," he continued, "you're not invited to the meeting."

Her pen clattered onto the table. "Why not?"

"After what happened in Chicago, I don't have a lot of faith in your judgment."

Sandra felt blood drain from her face, then flood back in mortification.

"You might earn that faith back," he said, "but for now, I'm keeping you in the back room."

Maybe she deserved that. But she was damned if she was going to stay *in the back room* a second longer than she had to.

"You still need to keep me informed about who you're talking to." She opened her folder. "Otherwise we could end up duplicating effort, and we don't have time for that." She passed a document over to him. "These are the companies I see as our top priorities to approach about sponsorship."

"I already tried Dollarwise Homes." He turned the page. "And Foremost Savings Bank."

"You see, I don't know that," she said, "because you don't tell me what you're doing."

He scowled. "You're getting repetitive."

"You're making me," she said, still smarting from his criticism. "And I'm sick of it."

"Too bad," he snapped. Then, inexplicably, he grinned. A wide, almost boyish grin that made him breathtakingly handsome. Sandra was glad she hadn't seen that back when she was young and impressionable. He began reading through the list again.

"There are some good names on here," he conceded. "I'll start making some calls."

She snatched the list from him. "If you ever get out of the sporting goods business, you could have a great career as a door."

He stared at her. "What are you talking about?"

"You're so good at shutting people out." She waved the document at him. "This is my work, I want to get involved. I thought we could agree on our approach, then divide the list in two. We'll get through it faster that way—assuming you can trust me with something as simple as a phone call," she added bitterly.

Taney looked at her as if she'd suggested they eat lug nuts for lunch. Then his brows knit together. "I appreciate what you've done here—" he grabbed the list off her before she even saw him coming "—but I'll make the calls."

"You said we're a team."

"Teams need a boss and I'm it."

"Teams need a leader," she corrected.

"Same thing."

How was she supposed to save her business when he wouldn't let her get a look in? Sandra stood, then stalked halfway across the room so she wouldn't punch him. "Why is Sunglass State a better sponsor for Will than International Sunglasses?" she demanded.

He sighed. "I could think of an answer, but I don't want to steal your thunder."

Steely-voiced, she said, "Because International Sunglasses' target demographic is much younger than Will. He's bang in the middle of Sunglass State's market."

"And your point is?"

"You're out of touch, Taney. You don't know the first thing about how Will fits with those companies' brand strategies." She nodded at the list. "You won't sign a sponsor if you can't demonstrate synergy with their brand. The price of a NASCAR Sprint Cup Series sponsorship might be measured in dollars, but the value is a whole lot more complex."

WHAT WAS IT ABOUT her voice that made him want to agree with whatever she said, Taney wondered. It was low and melodic, and listening to her on the phone, when he couldn't see her, drove him nuts. His efforts to resist the lure of that voice usually drove him too far in the opposite direction—he seldom actually agreed with her.

Ever since that fight, he'd been uncomfortably aware of his attraction her. But that didn't mean squat when it came to business, and in that arena, she'd blown her credibility. He was about to tell her that when he needed her input he'd ask for it, when Jack Carter strode into the room, which meant a premature end to what was shaping up to be a decent battle.

"Hey, pal, glad you could make it." Taney got up to shake Jack's hand. Jack couldn't take his eyes off Sandra, so Taney introduced them.

It was obvious Jack was impressed by her. Like Taney, he was six-four, which meant her height didn't faze him. Quite the opposite. He held on to her hand while he extended their greeting into pleasantries, until Taney was forced to direct his friend to a seat.

"Thanks, Sandra," he said, "you can go now."

She bridled at the dismissal. Then she gave Jack a dazzling smile and said, "Jack, I'd love to tell you some of my ideas for getting brand synergy out of a NASCAR sponsorship."

"I'd love to hear them," Jack said promptly, which was all Sandra needed to sit down again.

Didn't she listen to a word Taney said? Hadn't he ordered her to stay in the back room? But he couldn't throw her out now without causing a fuss.

Taney outlined in more detail the opportunity to sponsor Will. Sandra didn't interrupt until they got into a question-and-answer session, and some of that fell in to her court—naturally, she didn't hold back. Jack spoke warmly to her, grinned, bantered. She grinned and bantered right back. Taney found himself increasingly irritated, increasingly convinced of the attractions of shy, retiring women.

Still, he wasn't churlish enough to interrupt their cozy chat when the discussion was headed in the right direction. When Jack asked about return on investment, Taney said his piece about the dollars, then turned to Sandra. "How about you share some of your thoughts on brand synergy with Jack?" Since that was how she'd weaseled her way in here.

She leaned forward, which Taney knew would enhance her already impressive cleavage in that square-cut T-shirt. He watched Jack watching her, and saw Jack's gaze flick down and back with impressive speed. Taney felt a sudden dislike for his buddy—in fact, he couldn't remember why they'd become friends in the first place. And hadn't Jack cheated on his now ex-wife?

"The physical differences between the average basketball player and the average NASCAR driver might suggest there's no obvious synergy," Sandra said. "A six-foot-five basketball player wouldn't have much fun in a NASCAR Sprint Cup Series car, and a Cup driver isn't going to shine in the NBA."

Jack nodded, his eyes on Sandra's. She had an expressive face, even when she wasn't bawling out Taney.

"This is off the top of my head, because Taney didn't mention we were meeting today—" the reproach in her voice, directed at Taney, was a display of blatant nerve "—but from a marketing perspective, those differences are something we can build on."

"Sounds interesting," Jack murmured in a tone that suggested his next words would be an invitation to view his etchings. Sandra smiled innocently.

"It's not just that both sports require exceptional fitness and dedication to make it to the top," she said, "although those angles will come into any promotion." The way she flicked her hair back, then smiled, told Taney she was aware of Jack's interest and she intended to take advantage of it. "But I'm thinking, a pro basketball player always stands out in the crowd."

Jack nodded.

"So does a NASCAR Sprint Cup Series driver. Will Branch isn't yet a winner, but you'll see he has the kind of presence that makes people listen. If we align Will's ability to stand out in the crowd with a theme of Hoops And More helping players and teams to stand out, we might have a starting point for some great synergy."

It was a good idea, Taney conceded, especially since it was *off the top of her head*.

They wound up the discussion soon after that. Taney planned to take Jack down to pit road to see the team in action. Hopefully his friend would be fired up with the passion that led grown men to throw millions of dollars at a race team.

The kind of passion Taney used to have.

He didn't invite Sandra to join them—he'd had enough of watching Jack drool over her. But Jack wasn't ready to let go of the ball. He'd always had that problem, now Taney came to think of it.

"Sandra," Jack said, hanging on to her hand after he was finished shaking it, "how about I take you to dinner next time I'm in Charlotte?" He paused, then added, "Which could be next week, if you're free."

Taney felt a flicker of annoyed admiration. It took guts to ask a woman out in front of another guy—Jack must feel confident he and Sandra had made a connection.

But Taney was certain his friend had jumped the green flag there. No way could Sandra be interested in Jack, when there was this powerful undercurrent flowing between her and Taney.

To save his friend an embarrassing rejection, he said, "Sandra's pretty tied up the next couple of weeks. We're planning a lot of dinners with potential sponsors." For good measure he added, "And lunches."

Okay, he'd told Sandra she was in the back room. But he'd decided to reward her for doing so well in this meeting with Jack.

A discomfiting picture took shape in his mind. Sandra in her sexy but discreet low-cut tops, meeting with all those male marketing vice presidents and CEOs who might want to sign up for a sponsorship. They'd all be looking at her the way Jack did. To Taney, the process sounded fraught with tension. He wondered how she'd react if he suggested she tone down her wardrobe. Not well, if the way she reacted to just about everything else he said was any indication.

Sandra sent Taney a wide, pleased smile that sent a jolt

through him. Then she turned exactly the same smile on Jack. "Sounds as if I'll be pretty busy," she said. "But I have your number, so I'll call you if I have some spare time."

She *wanted* to go out with Jack?

Irritation burned in Taney's throat. He was running a business, not a dating agency. "Jack, why don't you go on ahead and say hello to Will, he's expecting you. Sandra and I need to plan next week's schedule."

It seemed Jack still had more of that flirtatious chitchat to get through. Taney was assailed by a sensation he wasn't sure he wanted to name, but wrapped up in there was the urge to punch Jack's lights out. And also, a compulsion to help Sandra put her jacket back on, then do up the buttons.

After Jack left, Taney forced himself to wait before he spoke, so he didn't do anything silly like forbid Sandra to date his friend.

"The discussion went pretty well," he said.

"Uh-huh." Sandra walked down through the tiered seating to the window and looked out over the track, with the annoying result that Taney couldn't see her face.

"I think Jack's keen," he said. "On the sponsorship deal."

"Maybe not as keen as you think."

Because obviously, Taney thought with a flash of annoyance when he remembered how she'd laughed and agreed with Jack, it would choke her to agree with Taney. "He's very interested," he said firmly. What was so fascinating out that window, anyway? Was she waiting for Jack to appear down below?

"He struck me as a little flaky," she said.

Taney relaxed. Perversely, he now felt compelled to

defend his friend. "Jack's a good guy, I've known him for years. I don't think he'd mislead me about this."

Sandra turned, leaned her back against the window. "Did you see the way his face closed up when we talked about money?"

"He doesn't like to show his hand," Taney said. "Neither do I."

"You can say that again," she muttered.

"Admit it," Taney said, more out of a desire to find out what she thought of Jack than because he believed it, "you're antsy about him because he asked you on a date."

She rolled her eyes. "That's garbage."

He walked down the stairs to stand right in front of her. "You said you'd call him. Did you mean it?"

"Why did you change your mind about me getting involved in the sponsor meetings?"

"Because you did a good job," he said impatiently. "Do you plan to call Jack?"

She sent him a long, measuring look. Then she said, "He's not my type."

Taney saw his friend down below, traversing the stands. Jack was tall, funny and, Taney was fairly certain, good-looking. A lot like Taney. "How not your type?" he asked.

SANDRA DECIDED it was time to disabuse Taney of his assumption that she liked him. Which he seemed to have reached without bothering to like her back. She folded her arms. "I'm not interested in six-foot-plus jocks."

She saw by the narrowing of his eyes that he'd gotten the message, loud and clear. He rubbed his chin in a way that suggested he was more intrigued than offended.

"So what is your type?" he asked.

"I can't imagine why you need to know that," she said smoothly, and headed back up the stairs. Down there by the window, she had no room to maneuver.

"Let's just imagine that I do," he countered, following her.

Since he'd asked for it, why not hammer home the fact that she wasn't interested? She poured herself a glass of water from the carafe on the table and took a delicate sip. "I like men who are more…emotionally intelligent. More sensitive."

Sensitive wasn't the right word, but she wasn't about to embarrass herself by admitting the truth, her secret dream. That six-foot, self-sufficient, independent businesswoman Sandra Jacobs wanted to be *cherished*.

Of all the antiquated, foolish notions.

She noted with satisfaction that Taney looked every bit as horrified as she'd assumed he would.

"You want some guy who lights smelly candles and plays sissy music while he cooks you vegetarian lasagna?"

She sputtered into her water glass. "You see, that's how I'd expect someone with low emotional intelligence to define sensitive."

He snorted. "And what makes you think a six-foot-plus jock can't be sensitive? How do you know that I, to use a random example—" the battle light in his eye told her there was nothing random about it "—am not an incredibly sensitive guy?"

"It's a vibe," she said snootily. "You don't have it."

He pffed. "Sensitive, my butt."

She raised an eyebrow to tell him his comment had reinforced his total lack of sensitivity.

He scowled. "You'd make mincemeat of a guy like that."

Sandra bristled. She hated it when people made judgments purely on her height. "Just because I'm tall, it doesn't mean I'm aggressive or...or manlike or..."

THREE STRIDES BROUGHT TANEY to her side. "Who said anything about *manlike?*" The way he loomed over her, there was no doubt who was the man here.

"When you're my height you sometimes get accused of trying to wear the pants."

Taney eyed her long legs in those slim-fitting black pants and couldn't see a damned thing wrong with the idea. He moved his gaze up to those gorgeous curves. "Manlike is the last thing any guy would think about you." He paused. "That is, any guy who's secure in his own masculinity. I can't speak for wimpy, sensitive—"

"I thought you wanted to plan next week's schedule, not criticize my taste in men," she said. "Until your friend comes through with an offer—" her tone said she didn't believe that would happen "—we have work to do."

"We'll do this your way," he said magnanimously, since he hadn't had a chance to think up a better way. "We'll divide the list down the middle, start setting up appointments. We'll keep in touch by e-mail to make sure we're not double-booked."

"If I may make a suggestion, assuming you're secure enough in your masculinity to listen..."

Crap. Taney had the sudden feeling he'd dug a hole for himself with his views on male sensitivity. "I'm secure," he growled.

"Let's keep in touch face-to-face. You need to be more visible at team HQ and at the races."

"I can't be everywhere," he said. "I have a business to

run and now a sponsor to find. Jason's in charge of the team—he goes to the races."

"Jason's a nice guy, but he's a paper pusher and he's too soft," she said. "You're the owner—people want to please you. I believe Will would race better if he knew you were there, and the team would do a better job of setting up the car. There's even a chance you could inspire them to win."

She didn't sound at all convinced of that last point, which had Taney's hackles rising. When he'd first started the team, the pep talks he'd dispensed on race day had been legendary. And they'd produced results. But that was back in the days when he couldn't wait to get in to the team headquarters each day, and enjoyed nothing more than spending time on the workshop floor with the guys.

These days, nothing appealed less. With the sudden possible exception of spending time with Jack Carter.

But maybe Sandra was right. Not about the team improving, he didn't believe a pep talk from him would be enough to lift Will above his current mediocrity, but Taney's increased visibility as an owner enjoying his team would remind sponsors of the perks of the deal, and would also serve his other, big-picture goal.

"I'll think about it," he said.

Sandra seemed to take that as outright agreement. Her perky, know-it-all smile suggested she expected to see him in the garage at every race.

He found himself admiring the way she stuck to her guns. Still, he wasn't quite sure what had happened here. Taney was used to things happening just the way he planned, and today, he'd planned to get those sponsor names from her, then send her away while he did the wheeling and dealing. Instead, he'd had to worry about

Jack harassing her, he'd agreed to run the sponsor search her way, he'd been dismissed as an insensitive jerk who wasn't her type and, at least in her mind, he'd promised to show up to a bunch of races he didn't want to go to.

How could she think she wanted a sensitive man? Anyone could see she needed a guy who'd give as good as she gave, with whom she could go chin-to-chin.

If Sandra ever got a sensitive man in her sights, Taney pitied the guy.

CHAPTER FIVE

THE NORTHERLY ASPECT of the Sunny Hills Rehabilitation and Senior Care Center's valley setting made a liar of whoever had chosen the name.

But it was one of the few facilities that catered to the needs of both of Sandra's parents and, in her estimation, was the best of its kind in the Charlotte area.

Thanks to the relative lull resulting from a two-week gap between races, she could fit in an extra visit to her folks. She pulled in to the parking lot on Tuesday morning in a much happier frame of mind than last time. She and Taney hadn't found a sponsor yet, but Taney was including her in his meetings, and he was willing to come to races. If Taney Motorsports performed better, the sponsors would come.

She locked her car and, as always, headed to see her father first.

The TV was on in his room in Sunny Hills' advanced care facility, and her dad was sitting in his brown checkered recliner, brought from home, watching a rerun of the race at Bristol. He'd watched it when she brought it last Friday, too—Sandra had sat with him through half of it. But he would have no memory of that now.

Sandra was certain he didn't follow the race, but something about the brightly colored NASCAR Sprint Cup Series cars, or maybe the noise, held his attention where nothing else could. He'd been a NASCAR fan more than fifty of his sixty-seven years, and she wondered if that was why the tapes still worked for him. He had a total lack of awareness of current events, and no short-term memory, but occasionally he revealed flashes of memory of his distant past. That past included hundreds of NASCAR races.

Sandra knew that some relatives of Sunny Hills' residents experimented with music therapy to decrease their loved ones' stress and reduce the outbreaks of agitated behavior common to Alzheimer's patients. She liked to think of her tapes as NASCAR therapy.

She bent over her father, kissed his forehead. He looked up at her, surprised.

"Hi, Dad. It's me, Sandra."

She was rewarded with a smile of vague recognition. Brendan Jacobs didn't know Sandra was his daughter, but he knew she was familiar, and that soothed him. If not her.

From the moment her dad had been diagnosed with Alzheimer's seventeen years ago, Sandra had known he would get to this stage…and worse. Knowing it never made the reality easier to accept.

She pulled a tape out of her bag. "I brought you the tape of Martinsville. Bart Branch had a great race."

"Good," her father said. His speech was no longer distinct and was limited to only a few syllables at a time.

Sandra stayed an hour, watching the race, enjoying the only connection she still shared with her dad. She felt bad having to leave…but he didn't even register her departure.

She crossed the quadrangle, heading for the independent

living apartment where her parents had been together until four years ago, when her father's condition had deteriorated to the extent her mom couldn't look after him anymore.

"Sandra." A voice hailed her from the front of the administration building to her left. Margaret Holden, general manager of Sunny Hills, stepped out of the reception area. "I saw your car in the parking lot, I thought I might find you in your father's room."

"I've already seen Dad." Sandra waited for the woman to catch her up. "I'm on my way to Mom. It's a flying visit."

"You're always so busy," the woman said approvingly.

"Did you want to talk about Dad?" Sandra asked. "Has there been any unexpected development?" The expectation was that her father would grow slowly, steadily worse. Those minor deteriorations didn't justify the staff contacting Sandra.

Margaret shook her head. "Nothing to do with your father's health, but bad news nonetheless." She handed Sandra a white envelope, sealed, with her name handwritten on the front. "I'm afraid our fees are going up."

"Up!" Sandra couldn't prevent the distressed exclamation. "But there was an increase just last year."

"I'm sorry." Margaret's mouth pressed together in a firm but not uncompassionate line. "The board has determined that for us to continue to provide the level of care we currently offer, we need to charge more."

Sunny Hills had never been the cheap option. After her dad had moved in to the hospital, leaving her mother alone in the apartment, the costs had risen considerably.

Never one to delay bad news, Sandra tore the envelope open, extracted the folded sheet of paper. Twelve percent. She groaned.

"I'm sorry, my dear," Margaret said. "This isn't going to be easy for any of our families." She glanced around, then leaned forward confidingly, "I suspect Mrs. Thompson's daughter will have to remove her mother, though where she'll find another place for her at this stage, I don't know."

That was the problem. There was a shortage of quality facilities. Most either offered retirement care or hospital care, not both. Those that did, were expensive, like Sunny Hills, or not of a standard that Sandra could leave her parents in and still sleep at night. Nor did she want to separate them. Her mom treasured the couple of hours she spent each day with her dad. And from a selfish perspective, it suited Sandra to have them both in one facility.

She stuffed the letter into her purse, said a gloomy goodbye to Margaret. Then she continued on to her mom's apartment, her steps slowed by reflection.

It was all very well to say she couldn't take her parents elsewhere. But she might not have a choice. If Bart's new sponsor came through, that would help. But unless Will found a sponsor soon, Sandra would have more chance of jumping behind the wheel of the No. 467 car and winning the NASCAR Sprint Cup Series herself than she would of paying the higher fees.

She would have to put aside the difficulties between her and Taney. The two of them had to make this work.

THE TESTING SESSION had helped the Taney Motorsports team. Although Will qualified only twenty-sixth for the race at Texas, he and the pit crew worked better together on race day, and he finished twelfth.

Taney and Sandra watched the race together from on top

of the pit box. Taney hadn't done that for a long time. Memory had diluted the intense thrill of the noise, the speed.

"You realize you can probably take the credit for Will's improvement," Sandra told Taney as they walked into the garage after the race.

He snorted. "Just by being here?"

"My staff work better when I'm watching."

She had a point.

"You looked as if you had a good time today," she said.

It was her usual kind of leading comment, where if he gave her an inch, she'd turn it into a mile-long shopping list of P.R. exercises. "I've had worse."

Naturally, she started grinning away as if he'd said it was the best day of his life. But luckily for him, before she could launch into her spend-more-money spiel, she caught sight of Richard Latimer, Bart's team owner, near the No. 475 car.

"I need to speak to Richard," she told Taney.

He walked with her, always happy to talk to the older man. Sandra stopped when they were about thirty feet away.

"What's up?" Taney asked. She looked upset, her color high, her teeth digging into her lower lip. He hadn't seen her like this before, not even when he'd fired her, which had just made her mad.

"Richard's talking to MacKay Lundgren."

"So?"

She shivered. "I can't go near that creep. He's a liar and a cheat."

Did she mean personally—was Lundgren an ex-boyfriend of hers?—or professionally? MacKay Lundgren had a reputation for cunning, aggression and hard-heartedness. His success in buying failing businesses and turning them around or stripping them for their assets had put him on all the rich lists. He might not be the most ethical of businessmen, but he hadn't, as far as Taney knew, done anything that would qualify him as a cheat.

"Lundgren is a savvy investor in a tough market," he said. "Sometimes, it's every man for himself."

Her disdainful look told him what she thought of that philosophy. "And you still say you're a team player?"

Latimer's conversation with Lundgren came to an end. The two men shook hands, then Lundgren turned to leave. When he saw Sandra, he gave a knowing smirk. Then he excused himself from Latimer and walked off.

"What was that about?" Taney asked.

SANDRA DIDN'T EVEN WANT to talk about that jerk. Ignoring Taney's question, she approached Richard Latimer and asked him how the hunt for a sponsor for Bart was going.

"EZ-Plus Software is certainly keen, and I'm hoping they'll sign soon," Latimer said. "Bart's race today might have helped." Will's twin had finished sixth. Latimer's kind blue eyes were worried as he regarded Sandra. "I can still make Bart confess to his part in that TV show, if you think it'll help Will."

Richard was such a gentleman, always honorable—the kind of guy who'd given NASCAR its reputation for fair play. Sandra and Taney had told him about the switch—and as far as Sandra could tell, he hadn't said a word to anyone else.

"Thanks, but that won't help either of us in the long run," Sandra said. "They'll both look stupid and deceitful. We just need those guys to grow up."

MacKay Lundgren couldn't think of anything more tedious than watching cars drive around in circles for hours at a stretch, and the race he'd just watched had confirmed that view. No matter that every so often they smacked into the wall or each other, a car was a car and who gave a damn which was fastest.

But there were many people who disagreed with him, going by today's sellout crowd. Millions more across the country would be glued to their TV sets to watch the race.

NASCAR was a marketer's dream.

MacKay had dreams—or rather, ambitions—of making a killing in the auto finance market. And research showed that many of the people who borrowed money to purchase cars were NASCAR fans. So he'd put aside his lack of interest and turned up at the Texas track to start sniffing out the right sponsorship opportunity. Right equaled cheapest.

He'd uncovered a couple of good leads already, and he'd been about to start probing Richard Latimer for a price on Bart Branch's sponsorship package when he'd seen Sandra Jacobs. He had no desire to encounter her, so he'd excused himself from Richard and headed for the air-conditioned cool of the suite where he'd finagled an invitation to a post-race party. This was more like it—much more his speed than the garage area.

He snagged a fancy European beer from the bar and headed for the knot of men standing above the banked seating.

Halfway there, he saw *her*.

The suite wasn't that big, so he couldn't think how he'd missed her, except she was slim and the guy she was talking to was the wrong side of two hundred and fifty pounds.

MacKay changed course.

"Alyssa Ritchie," he drawled as he got closer.

She stiffened—he knew a burst of satisfaction that she recognized his voice after so long—and turned her head a fraction in acknowledgment.

"Hello, MacKay," she said coolly, seeming reluctant to deflect her attention from the oaf who was leering at her curves, displayed to advantage in a low-cut, clingy gold top.

Obviously, the guy made more money than MacKay.

MacKay inserted himself between them. "I haven't seen you in, what, five years?" His gaze flicked to her impressive cleavage. "You've worn them well. Who would guess you're over—"

"Excuse me, Wayne," she said to the oaf, "while I catch up with an old *friend*." She gave MacKay a little shove, and he allowed it to move him a few feet. He was quite happy to have Alyssa to himself.

As soon as she was out of Wayne's earshot, she dropped the dulcet tone. "Don't bother me, MacKay."

"I meant it," he said. "You look incredible." Just as incredible as he remembered. Her hair had been bleached that exact same color when he'd first met her seventeen years ago. She'd been Hilton Branch's gorgeous young mistress—MacKay had been one of very few people who'd suspected the affair. Back then MacKay had been on his first wife. *Times change.*

Alyssa reminded MacKay of Suzanne, wife number one. Suzanne had looked almost as luscious—and been almost as hard and selfish. She'd tried to fleece him, but MacKay had managed to divorce her without paying her a penny. Alyssa was much smarter—over the years she'd reportedly accrued a small fortune from Hilton and her other lovers.

MacKay didn't know why—when he could barely remember what Suzanne looked like—he could never forget Alyssa.

"If that's all you wanted to say," she said, "I guess we're done."

"I didn't know you had a personal interest in NASCAR," MacKay said. "Enough to keep you coming to the track now that Hilton's abandoned you."

ALYSSA WOULD HAVE loved to stomp her stiletto on MacKay's foot. But Hilton Branch had taught her to behave better than that—in public, anyway.

And every woman in this suite was already laughing at her, now that Hilton had taken his millions and run off without his mistress. She didn't need to give them any more food for gossip.

"Actually, I'm a big fan," she said. No one had been more surprised than she to find it was true. When Hilton became interested in NASCAR, she'd gone along to the races—Hilton had arranged tickets for her and whatever harmless man she brought along as her "date." She'd expected to be frustrated to be out in public with Hilton yet forced to hide her status as his mistress. But it hadn't been a problem—from day one, she'd been seduced by NASCAR, by the speed, the skill, the power.

And the money.

"But I haven't seen you at a race before," she said.

"My first time," MacKay said. "But now that I know you're a regular…"

"Don't bother," she snapped.

MacKay was probably the best-looking man in the room, but she wasn't interested. She made a point of never dating men worth less than a million dollars. MacKay had many millions, but at heart, he was dirt poor. She didn't know what ditch he'd scrabbled his way out of, but she sensed there was one somewhere in his past, and that was too close for her.

She'd met him in the days when she'd been in love with Hilton—so neither she nor MacKay had acknowledged or acted on the instant, undeniable chemistry between them. The chemistry had been present at every encounter in the intervening years, which was why she never spent time alone with him. He was too sharp, too clever, too much of an opportunist.

Too much like her.

"I thought you might be on the hunt for a new man to fund your lifestyle," he said.

Despite his obvious interest, she knew he wasn't offering. MacKay would never have to buy female attention. "You're right, of course," she said. Because her true ambition was no business of MacKay's. "Plenty of rich pickings around here." Her gaze flicked over him the way his had over her earlier. "But I can't see anyone in the immediate vicinity worth passing the time of day with, so if you'll excuse me…"

Before she could execute a perfect heel-turn, MacKay grabbed hold of her arm. She looked down at his fingers, registered their strength against her bare flesh.

"Do you realize this is the first time in seventeen years that we've met while we've both been single?" His thin, sexy mouth curved in a smile.

"Someone's keeping count," she said, secretly pleased.

"Have dinner with me tonight."

There was no denying she was tempted. But Alyssa had plans, and MacKay Lundgren was no use to her. She lifted his hand off her arm. "Sorry, MacKay, you can't afford me."

TANEY PLEASANTLY surprised Sandra with his enthusiasm when he talked to potential sponsors about NASCAR. For a guy who didn't seem to care about his team, he had a lot to say, all of it passionate.

When he spoke about the thrill of watching his driver battle through a NASCAR Sprint Cup Series race, his hazel eyes lit up, he smiled more and laugh lines Sandra hadn't known existed showed up around his mouth. She couldn't believe Taney was lying to sponsors about his feelings—like his NASCAR Sprint Cup–winning team-building skills, that passion for the sport was inside him somewhere. It was her job to unearth it, so that the team—and its publicity—would resume their rightful position at the top of his priority list.

A couple of the companies they approached about sponsorship had female vice presidents of marketing, and Sandra noticed how they responded to Taney's guarded charm. To his credit, Taney was never less than completely professional with them. Any non-NASCAR talk stayed at the surface level—and not a flirtatious surface. When he and Sandra met with men, as was more often the case, Taney's social discourse was invariably about sports—all sports, not just NASCAR. Again, very surface, but Sandra could see that other people liked and respected him.

She and Taney made a good team. They filled in the

gaps in each other's presentations, coming across as united in their enthusiasm for the team. But they disagreed with each other enough—occasionally to the point of public argument—that people trusted them more than they would a supersmooth pitch.

It was just as well they were compatible from a business perspective, as often they were together all day, moving from meeting to meal to meeting to meal.

Small wonder Sandra found it increasingly hard to ignore Taney. Or rather, to ignore her awareness of him—it wasn't possible to altogether ignore six foot four of handsome male with a knack for dry jokes and an insistence on supporting her Krispy Kreme habit. That was the good side of Taney. The bad side was his high-handed approach to just about everything.

Sandra knew, even if he didn't, that Motor Media Group's future rode on the success of their working partnership, so it was hard when he insisted on calling the shots about who they met and what deal they offered. Sandra's objections had led to some rip-roaring arguments, which she'd started to realize he, like her, found to be a bizarre form of stress relief. A bellowed, "I'm the boss," was one of his favorite lines, often followed by, "Beats me why a smart lady like you can't seem to remember that."

Sandra knew he intended a backhanded compliment, but she was hypersensitive to any suggestion that she might be forgetful. His comment usually ended up inflaming the argument further.

That spark between them had an overall positive effect on their meetings with sponsors. But the reality was, they still hadn't achieved their goal.

"I don't understand why we haven't signed a sponsor

yet," she said to Taney during a Tuesday afternoon
progress review in the meeting room he'd commandeered
for his use at the team headquarters. "I know Hilton's
crime doesn't help our cause, but we've worked so hard
to distance Will from the scandal."

Restless, she stood and paced the short distance to the
window that overlooked the Taney Motorsports workshop.
Below them, the team was preparing the No. 467 car for
Saturday's race at Phoenix. The car would leave for the
track tomorrow.

Before Taney could comment, her cell phone rang. She
excused herself to take the call—Taney knew she had to
be always available to the media.

"Dr Zakursky." Darn! "I'm so sorry, but—"

"You forgot," the doctor said.

"Yes. I mean, I put the appointment in my diary, but
I...forgot to check it."

"This appointment was your idea," he reminded her
gently.

"I know, I'm sorry. Let's reschedule."

When she ended the call, Taney said, "Are you sure
you're not sick?" He sounded worried. Probably because
if she was ill, she wouldn't be able to put in the long hours
this sponsor search demanded.

Sandra forced a smile. "You don't want to know about
women and their doctors' appointments, do you?"

He blanched. "Hell, no. Let's get back to business." His
own phone rang, but, unlike her, he never seemed to
answer it. He glanced at the display and switched the
phone off. "Where were we?"

"I was about to say we're doing a fabulous job." Sandra
parted the vertical blinds so she could get a better look at

the No. 467 car, the large number emblazoned on its hood—the prime real estate space that should be occupied by a sponsor name.

"Fabulous, huh?" He spoke right behind her and, startled, Sandra spun to face him. She pressed a hand to her heart; his eyes followed the movement.

"That's your professional assessment, I assume?" He was frowning the half frown that meant he was looking forward to disagreeing with her. She'd never known someone who enjoyed contention as much as Taney did. He would argue that NASCAR races should be run clockwise, just for the hell of it.

"My incredibly accurate professional assessment," she insisted. "Taney, when we're in those meetings, we're hotter than a Texas racetrack in July."

It was an innocuous statement. But something—maybe her use of the word *hotter*—charged the air between them so that it hung full and heavy, like an imminent electrical storm.

Like a storm after a drought.

Dry-mouthed, Sandra licked her lips, saw Taney watching.

"Hotter," he said distractedly.

"Uh, yes. But for some reason, people aren't biting."

Biting wasn't a good word, either. What was wrong with her? She dragged her gaze from his lips, his teeth bared in a slow intimate smile she'd never seen before, one that made her think about…biting…and more.

"What you're saying," he said thoughtfully, "is that even though we're on fire in those meetings—" Sandra knew she wasn't imagining the heat in the room "—we can't convince anyone to get in to bed with us."

Dammit, he was doing that deliberately! Her shocked gaze met his eyes…and saw laughter, a wholly unexpected playfulness, lighting their hazel depths.

Even more unexpected was the lurch of hunger deep inside her.

CHAPTER SIX

"TANEY, I'M NOT SURE. What are you...?" For a woman who considered herself a supreme communicator, she was hideously tongue-tied. She stepped back, putting some distance between them. She took a swig from the glass of water she'd left on the table, eyed him warily over the rim.

Taney's smile turned rueful.

"We're both adults, Sandra, both old enough to know what's going on here."

"What, uh, do you mean?" *If we're both adults, why do I sound like a teenager?*

"And probably old enough to know better," he continued. "But given we've spent pretty much every waking hour together the past two weeks..."

Did he have to say "waking"? It made her think of sleeping, of bed.

"We've had breakfast, lunch and dinner together most days...."

"Usually with other people." She put her glass down and moved back to the window so she could see "other people," so she could remind herself this wasn't some hothouse little world just for the two of them. "With our sponsor prospects."

"We have similar goals, similar attitudes. Our physical

attributes are similar, and yet—" his gaze roamed her face, touched on the *V* of her jersey wrap top, moved back up to hold her eyes "—entirely complementary."

Those last words came out husky, and a mini heat wave scorched through Sandra.

"Small wonder we're attracted to each other," he said.

One part of her wanted to punch the air. He'd admitted he felt it, too. But that meant admitting that the attraction she thought she'd done such a great job of rooting out was flourishing.

She'd never been attracted to a client before. There must be a dozen good reasons why it was a bad idea. And she really, truly didn't like six-foot-plus jocks. Not at all.

"It's not like you to have nothing to say." Amusement deepened Taney's voice. Was it her imagination, or had he inched closer?

Sandra took a tiny step back and came up against the vertical blinds, which rustled and clattered. She wasn't going to play teenage games with him and lie about the attraction. But nor was she about to encourage him. "For once in my life, I'm saying nothing, and I'm going to pretend you did the same."

The curve of his mouth was more pronounced on the right side, she noticed. It lent a wryness to his smile.

"You disappoint me. I'm used to you bending my ear whether I want to hear it or not."

That was one thing she liked about Gideon Taney. He listened. She'd learned that over the past two weeks, and there was no doubt it was one of his most attractive qualities. Even when she thought her words had fallen on deaf ears, or he'd bellowed a refusal to one of her suggestions, he'd ask a question later that told her not only had she had his full attention, but he was also actually thinking about what she'd said.

But now, there was no talking. They seemed to be locked in a stare, their eyes conveying things that neither of them wanted to put into words.

Taney reached past her, and Sandra managed not to flinch. He tugged swiftly on the cord, and the vertical blinds swished shut, blocking out the workshop below.

"Taney…"

His smile held warmth, devilry and something almost tender. "Don't worry, the guys will think I'm firing you again."

His hand rested on the wall behind her, not exactly hemming her in, but to get away she'd first have to move closer to him, then squeeze past on the other side. Maybe if she'd been shorter—or less attracted to him—she'd have found his stance aggressive or intimidating. As it was, she felt the craziest urge to turn her head and rub her cheek against his strong wrist.

She contented herself with a close-up view of his arm, tanned and muscular, out of the corner of her eye. He must spend time outdoors, to be so tan in springtime.

And still he was looking at her intently, searching her face as if he could read her mind. Given her mind was operating at a particularly shallow level right now, he wouldn't need to look too deep.

Sandra closed her eyes for a long moment, didn't open them until she was sure she could hide just how much he consumed her thoughts.

When she looked back at Taney, his smile had widened and he was so close she would only have to move a fraction to be up against him.

"I think we should resume our meeting." Her voice came out breathy—even she thought it sounded like a come-on.

He thought about that for a moment, and again, he looked so playful, it was a shock. He shook his head.

Darn it, he'd definitely moved closer. How did such a large man do that, make those imperceptible movements that brought his lean length so near she could see the weave of his charcoal-gray polo shirt and the little creases at the corners of his mouth?

The smile left his face, to be replaced by an intensity that might have unnerved her if he'd forced her to meet his gaze. But it was her mouth that held his attention, and under the heat of that look, Sandra felt as if her lips bloomed fuller.

Taney lowered his mouth to hers, and it was all she could do not to cry out at the sizzle of contact. His lips were warm, firm, expert. With the same assuming arrogance he applied to everything, he demanded her cooperation. When Sandra parted her lips, he didn't hesitate to take advantage of her opening. But as soon as he gained the inside of her mouth, the nature of his quest changed. Still demanding, but no longer pushing. More inviting. If it was possible to be both urgent and leisurely, Taney's kiss was both.

His hands settled at Sandra's waist as he angled his head to deepen the kiss. Her arms found their way around his neck. Any second now, she would end this, but she'd waited so long, and the feel of him against her—strong, solid, seductive—cried out to be enjoyed another moment. Or two.

It was a long time since she'd kissed a man. An eternity since she'd kissed one like Taney.

She became aware of her body crushed against his.

Everything about him was so big, it made her want to yield to his strength, to the protection inherent in his hold. She moved against him, molded herself to his form.

Taney pulled back, broke the kiss. His arms stayed around her, but loosely. "I guess that had to happen." He sounded shaken.

"Uh-huh."

"That was incredible, even better than I expected." He kissed her forehead.

"Uh-huh."

"You know," he said quizzically, "I like you better when you're yelling at me. *Uh-huh* doesn't tell me much."

"Mmm," she said.

He gave her a little shake. "Speak to me, Sandra. Given I thought that kiss was fantastic and we never agree, you probably thought it was horrible."

She sighed. "Not horrible."

"You've got to stop paying me these extravagant compliments," he said.

She smiled. "It was great."

He made a little sound of frustration. "I suppose that'll do for now. Next time, I expect to hear, at the very least, amazing."

She eased out of his embrace. "There shouldn't be a next time."

"There damn well should." He grabbed her hand, as if to hold on to her. "I don't see how we can stop. Not when you dress so provocatively in the office."

"What the heck do you mean?" she said, indignant.

Mischief glinted in his eyes and she realized he was trying to prod her into a reaction.

"You don't know what these tight skirts do to me." He whisked her into his arms again. "Not to mention the sight of your incredibly erotic knees."

She smacked his shoulder. "You're sick."

His hands moved up, warming her through the silk of her blouse. One finger traced the skin at the *V* opening. Sandra caught her breath.

"Unquestionably provocative," he chided.

"To be any less *provocative,*" she said, "I'd have to dress like a nun."

He groaned, and slid a hand around the back of her neck. "Temptress! That mysterious black habit, that rare glimpse of an ankle…"

Her neck arched into his touch. "You really *are* sick."

He chuckled, then kissed her again. This time, Sandra ended it.

"Taney, I'm serious. I wanted to kiss you. But just once. We need to work together and doing this—" she moved her hand between them "—will complicate things."

He didn't look happy, but nor did he launch into a blustering argument. *He knows I'm right.* So why didn't she feel pleased?

"So we're agreed?" she said.

"You forget, I never agree with you." He pulled the cord to open the blind. "I haven't decided this is over—and I'm the boss."

That those words thrilled her probably meant she had serious domination issues. "You don't want to date me," she said, "because you'll never hear the end of my pleas for money."

He winced. "Sandra, there's something I haven't told you."

Just like that, her incoming disaster sensors blinked full alert.

"You do a great job for Taney Motorsports, but when I said I'm never going to increase the budget, I meant *never.*" He raked a hand through his hair and met her gaze square on. "I'm selling the team."

SHE WAS SO SILENT, so still, Taney wondered if she'd heard.

"No!" The exclamation burst out of her, propelled by an urgency he couldn't fathom. The intimacy of that kiss evaporated; she stared at him as if he'd betrayed her. It was his team, dammit, he could sell if he wanted.

"You can't," she said. Because as he'd just said, they never agreed, and if they ever did, it would likely signal the end of life as they knew it.

Taney called himself all kinds of fool. He hadn't meant to tell her about the sale until it was a done deal. But with the taste of her still seared on his lips, with the memory of her curves imprinted on the length of him, anything less than one hundred percent honesty had been impossible.

"Taney, why?" It was almost a moan.

He could tell this was going to get messy, and he had no idea why. He hated that kind of thing. *I shouldn't have kissed her.* But how could he not have?

He sat down, putting the table between them, and gestured to her to do the same. After a moment, she complied.

"You were right that day in Chicago," he said. "I haven't given enough time to racing in recent years, and this season has been the worst."

"I didn't mean you should sell," she protested, her face pale.

"The team's been on the market, quietly, for a couple of months. In Chicago, I signed an agreement with a buyer, subject to securing new sponsorship for Will. Which I thought I had."

She ignored his reference to the Olivia Winton debacle.

"But things are getting better," she pleaded. "The atmosphere in the team…I'm certain the results will follow."

He couldn't understand why she looked and sounded so devastated. "Sandra, I'm not interested in the team. I'm not getting anything out of it, I don't want to put any more in."

"It works the other way around," she said fiercely. "You put in, then you get something out."

Couldn't she ever just accept what he told her?

"This isn't up for discussion. I had several great years in NASCAR, but it's over. I don't have the passion for it, I want to move on to something else."

"What else is there?"

He shrugged. "I don't know yet." *But there must be something out there that will give me what I need.* "I can't pursue anything until the team is off my hands." Speaking of hands, she was twisting her fingers with worry. "Why is this such a big deal to you?"

"Here's the first thing that happens when a team changes hands," she said. "The new owner brings in his own people—and *fires* people like me."

Taney had to admit, he'd do that himself. Usually when you bought a business you had a bunch of ideas for how to improve it, and you wanted people you knew and trusted to implement them. "That may not happen."

And if it did…surely she didn't expect him to hang on to a dream that was long past its expiration date, just so she wouldn't lose the account?

"You'll find another client," he said. "I'll write a glowing recommendation."

"Why can't you just stick with the team, make it work so that you fall in love with it again?"

Fall in love? Taney shied away from the thought. "It's not about falling in love." Not with racing. Not with anything. Not with anyone. "This is business, I have to do what's best for me."

"Every man for himself?" she said. "Like MacKay Lundgren?"

She was trying to rile him—Taney knew he had a lot more integrity than Lundgren. He didn't give her the satisfaction, just said, "If you like, yes."

"That might be your motto," she said, "but mine is *never quit.*" She drew a long breath. "You can forget any thought of kissing me again. I don't date quitters."

SANDRA PULLED OUT of Wednesday's sponsor appointments with Taney. When he accused her of sulking, she said, "I can't see us impressing sponsors when it's clear we don't get along."

"You're being childish," he snapped.

It wasn't the kind of picking-a-fight-just-for-fun insult she'd come to appreciate. He sounded like the old Taney again, The Man Who Would Be Boss.

It was stupid to feel betrayed, as if in that one kiss he'd committed to share more than his lips with her, then immediately pulled that commitment out from under her. He didn't owe her anything.

She knew she would have to cooperate, once she'd finished sulking. Sure, Taney might not be able to sell the team if she didn't help him find a new sponsor. But nor

could he pay Motor Media Group to promote Will. Her
best bet was to help him find a sponsor, in the faint hope
the new owner would keep the existing P.R. arrangements.

There was one other option, she realized, as she
scanned her diary on Thursday afternoon and remembered
she was meant to be dining with Taney and the sponsorship manager from Beefy Burgers that night.

She could convince Taney not to sell the team.

Was that possible?

Why not? Persuading people to change or adopt a par-
ticular point of view was Sandra's job, and she was one of
the best. He already had an agreement to sell the team, but
he might have an out clause. What would it take to
convince him to exercise it?

Her phone rang, interrupting her plotting—the caller
was an attorney in Charlotte.

"My client is interested in sponsoring Will Branch,"
Mark Green said.

Still mired in her worries about Taney, it took Sandra a
moment to absorb the good news coming out of the blue.
"Um, that's great." One of the pitches she and Taney had
given must have paid off. She grabbed a pen and paper.
"Sounds like we need to schedule a meeting."

"A *confidential* meeting," the lawyer said. "Ms. Jacobs,
my client, who does not at this stage wish to be named,
has requested specifically that you should attend the
meeting, and that Gideon Taney cannot."

A small flash of triumph zapped through Sandra—any
victory over Taney had a sweetness to it. But the lawyer's
words didn't make sense. She sat back in her chair. "Taney
owns the team," she said slowly. "I don't have the authority to make a deal."

"My client wishes to discuss the options with you first, before involving Mr. Taney. Is that acceptable?"

She should have said no. Hadn't she bawled out Taney on more than one occasion for keeping information from her? But that was before she knew he planned to sell the team. Before he'd made it clear he'd been working behind her back. *Every man for himself.* She owed it to *her*self and to Will—even to Taney—to check out any potential sponsor.

She said, "When do you want to meet?"

They agreed a time the following Wednesday.

"I'll send over a pack of information for your client to read beforehand, including some ideas about how to measure return on sponsorship investment," Sandra said.

She packed her briefcase for her dinner meeting and headed to Taney Motorsports with only the tiniest twinge of conscience about concealing the new sponsor from Taney.

As SANDRA PULLED in to the Taney Motorsports parking lot—so studded with performance cars that it looked like an auto club meet—a truck swung by the front steps and stopped.

A girl—in her early teens, Sandra judged—hopped down from the passenger side. The driver waved as he left, but the girl, whose brown backpack looked too heavy for her shoulders, wasn't looking. She had her eyes fixed on the two-story brick-and-glass Taney Motorsports building, her head thrown back so she could take it all in at once.

Shouldn't she be in school? Coming up behind her, Sandra murmured, "Hi." The girl jumped and wheeled to face Sandra.

She was the spitting image of Taney. Aside from her definite femininity, though even that was tomboyish in those skinny jeans, black T-shirt and Will Branch signature ball cap. The resemblance lay in the wide-set hazel eyes, the oval face and a chin that promised a royal battle if its owner didn't get her own way.

"You must be related to Gideon Taney," Sandra said.

She nodded. "He's my uncle."

Taney had family? Of course he would, but somehow, Sandra had never envisaged him with relatives.

"Do you work here?" the girl asked.

"More often than not." Sandra smiled. "I do publicity for the team."

The girl glanced away. "Is Taney in? My dad said he's based at the team headquarters these days."

How strange that even his niece called Taney by his surname. "I have a meeting scheduled with him now." Sandra stepped forward, and the automatic door glided open. "I'll show you where to find him."

"Good of you to come back," Taney said sourly when she walked in to the meeting room. But he stood with his usual courtesy and relieved her of her heavy briefcase. Then he proceeded to argue with her as if they hadn't kissed, as if she hadn't refused to date him, as if he hadn't dealt her business a mortal blow.

"I've been thinking about your suggestion that we approach Fresher Flowers," he said, "and you're wrong."

He was treating their sponsor hunt as something entirely separate from all those other things. How could he compartmentalize his life like that?

Sandra tried to convey that entire thought process— which could be summarized as *you jerk*—to him in a concentrated glare. His eyebrows shot up, his lips twitched. Before he could say anything, she stepped aside to reveal his niece behind her.

"Danielle." After a double take, Taney came around the desk. "What are you doing here?"

"I thought I could stay with you awhile," Danielle said. She scowled at Sandra in a way that was obviously intended to tell her to make herself scarce. She looked so like Taney, Sandra had to bite back a smile. Since Taney didn't object to Sandra's continued presence, she headed for the table and sat down, happy to watch a Taney-to-Taney encounter. It might prove educational.

Taney looked around. "Where's your dad?"

"At home," Danielle said with studied casualness.

"At home in *Boston?*"

Sandra's jaw dropped. Danielle was a runaway?

The girl nodded.

"And your mom?"

"At home." A mumble.

"How did you get here?" he demanded, aghast.

"On a plane." The girl obviously preferred the pulling-teeth approach to answering questions.

"Who bought the ticket?"

"I did."

"How did you pay for it?" he said suspiciously.

Danielle licked her lips. "I used Mom's credit card."

Yikes. "Who was that guy who dropped you off outside the building?" Sandra inserted. Taney's face grew thunderous.

Another angry scowl. "I sat next to him on the plane. He was nice."

Taney swore furiously, heedless of his niece's tender

ears. "Your parents don't know you're here, do they?" He strode to his desk.

"Yes, they do."

Taney stopped. "They do?"

Sandra wanted to laugh. Danielle could charge good money for lessons in how to handle Taney.

"You left your parents a note," she guessed.

THE TEEN jerked a nod.

"A note!" Taney grabbed the phone, began dialing. What the hell was Dani thinking? His brother and sister-in-law would be out of their minds. "Steve, it's me. Danielle's here."

He didn't get to say another word for a whole minute, while his usually mild-mannered brother lambasted him for not answering his cell phone.

Oh, yeah. Steve had called a few times this afternoon, but Taney had been too busy to pick up.

"Steve, I'm sorry." He managed to get a word in edgewise. "You know she's safe now, so how about I call you back when I've figured out a plan to get her home to you?" He returned Danielle's frown measure for measure.

When he ended the call, Danielle said, "I don't want to go back."

"Of course you do," he growled.

She shook her head. "Not until Mom and Dad agree to be reasonable."

"You have the most reasonable parents in the world and they want you home, who knows why. Anyway, I can't look after you." How old was Danielle now? Taney guessed thirteen. She was no longer a kid he could fob off with a pat on the head and a candy bar. "Why don't you play on the computer while I book your flight home?"

"No way," was the unpromising reply.

Sandra sent him an accusing look that suggested he was handling this all wrong. "I can't look after her," he reiterated.

"Perhaps you should talk to Danielle about why she wants to be with you rather than her parents," she suggested.

"I will talk to her. On the way to the airport." Steve and Lisa were great parents, so there couldn't be any real problem. Maybe Danielle had boyfriend troubles—though wasn't thirteen a little young for that? If she did, Taney definitely wasn't the best person for her to talk to.

"Don't I get a say in this?" Danielle folded her arms and stuck out her chin. She plunked herself down on a chair and pressed herself into it, as if she wouldn't be moved. Taney wondered if Steve would approve of him manhandling her into the car.

"You should at least plan to spend some time with her first," Sandra said.

"Yeah." Danielle dragged her chair closer to Sandra's, her hostility vanishing in an instant change of allegiance. *Thank you very much, Ms. Know-It-All.*

"We have a dinner with Beefy Burgers," he reminded her.

"We can reschedule. Why don't you book Danielle on a late flight home, and have an evening with her? Family is important."

Hours of one-on-one time with his niece... Taney couldn't imagine what they might talk about that wouldn't be awkward. But Danielle's eyes glowed, making her look younger and reminding Taney she was his favorite niece. His only niece. Maybe Sandra had a point.

Besides, things hadn't exactly ended well between the two of them the other day. He assumed Sandra's presence here meant she was over her unreasonable reaction to him selling the team. But it wouldn't hurt to take her advice, if he had an eye to kissing her again. Which he most definitely did.

"Only if you come, too," he told Sandra. It was the perfect solution. She'd be a buffer between him and Danielle, and once they'd put Dani on a plane, he'd be alone with Sandra. Late at night.

"No, thank you." To Danielle, she said, "I'm sure you're a lot of fun, sweetie, it's Taney who bores me to tears."

Taney fixed Sandra with a disbelieving stare—*were those boredom noises you were making when my hands were all over you?*—but she tilted her chin so that it matched Danielle's for uppityness.

Dani giggled. She obviously liked Sandra and had a downer on anyone called Taney at the moment. All the more reason for Sandra to help him out here.

"Come with us, Sandra," he ordered. As if that would make her comply. He cast around for something to sweeten the deal. "After we take Danielle into the airport, you can tell me why I shouldn't sell the team."

It was a throwaway line, but it hit pay dirt. Sandra's lips maintained a vaguely contemptuous sneer, but her blue eyes gleamed with a betraying interest. So, she planned to talk him out of selling the team, huh? Taney wondered why. Surely his account couldn't be that important to her? There was no way he would change his mind, but no need to remind her of that.

"I suppose I could come along," she said.

CHAPTER SEVEN

TANEY TOLD SANDRA they might take Danielle to BamBam, a hip restaurant in uptown Charlotte.

"You don't want to encourage her to think you're more fun than her parents," Sandra pointed out. "Take her to your house for beans on toast."

"I hate beans on toast." He glanced at his niece, who'd left the meeting room to hang precariously over the balustrade above the workshop. "But that's smart thinking. We'll go to my place and I'll barbecue."

"It's not even sixty degrees outside."

He grinned. "After five minutes she'll be hankering for her mom's nice warm kitchen."

"Cruel and unusual," Sandra said approvingly.

But like her uncle, Danielle wasn't easily deflected. She loved the idea of a barbecue. And Taney's home on Lake Norman wasn't exactly a hovel that would compare unfavorably to her parents' place. The stone-and-timber house—mansion—set yards from the lake's edge was gorgeous.

Inside, it was spacious but somehow cozy. Taney pointed out the gym, sauna and indoor pool that catered to the fitness fanatic, but Sandra preferred the living spaces—open-plan rooms with deep carpet underfoot and high, timbered ceilings. The kitchen's combination of woodsy welcome and granite-and-steel efficiency would please everyone from a top chef to a grandma cooking pot roast.

"This place is incredible, Taney," Sandra said as she shivered beside him at the grill on the deck overlooking the lake. He'd lent her one of his sweaters, an ecru cable-knit that smelled of detergent mixed with Taney's clean, male scent. The sweater dwarfed her, but she hadn't quite warmed up yet.

They sat down to ribs and salad—mercifully inside, at the enormous rough-hewn dining table.

For a few minutes there was silence to allow apprecia-tion of the tender, smoke-flavored meat. Then Sandra sent Taney a loaded look.

He took a swig of his beer and appeared to brace himself. "What's the problem, Dani?"

Danielle had been laughing and joking with them, but, recalled to her woes, she slumped down in her seat. "I want to race a quarter midget, but Dad won't let me."

Taney frowned. "That doesn't sound like your dad. I thought he'd love to see you on the dirt."

"He lets Josh race a go-kart." Danielle pouted; Sandra assumed Josh was her brother. "But he thinks it's too dan-gerous for a girl. How am I ever going to race the NASCAR Sprint Cup Series if I can't get into a race car without Dad freaking out?"

Taney choked on his beer. "I didn't know you want to race NASCAR."

"Of course I do." She made it sound as if any other career choice was preposterous. "Taney, will you ask Dad for me?"

He picked up a meaty rib. "I guess I could."

"When?"

"When I get time."

"Very soon," Sandra told her.

He frowned at her. "But don't expect your dad to put you behind the wheel tomorrow," he warned Dani. "You need to face the consequences of stealing your Mom's money to fly down here—yes, it was stealing," he said, as Dani made to protest. "Why didn't you just call me to talk about this?"

"I did call," she said. "I left four messages on your answering machine here and one at your office."

And Taney hadn't replied. Typical, Sandra thought.

"Next time, threaten to fly down, and I promise I'll get right back to you," he said.

After dessert—ice cream and store-bought apple pie, which Dani declared to be nowhere near as good as her mom's—they drove to the airport.

Then it was just Taney and Sandra for the ride home.

"You were great with Danielle," Taney said as they waited at a red light. He leaned across and brushed a kiss over Sandra's mouth, before she could remember to say "No quitters."

Her lips tingled; she decided to ignore the kiss. "All I did was take an interest—it wasn't difficult when she's such a strong-minded kid."

"You'd be a good mom."

Tick-tick. Great, he'd just wound up her biological clock, which she'd recently managed to ignore, and now she had that hollow, dissatisfied feeling inside her, no matter that she was full of ribs and apple pie.

Stop, she told herself. No more thinking about biological clocks, no more thinking about Taney, no more thinking about that kiss two days ago, when she'd plastered herself to him like a tear-off to a windshield.

Because how could she convince him not to sell the team if her mind wasn't on the job? She eyed Taney's hands on the steering wheel. Strong, long-fingered, no rings. Why couldn't he be married, so she wouldn't even think about him?

Instead, she had to tolerate the fact that every glance, every casual touch, added another twig to a potential conflagration. She turned to look out her window, as if she might discern the passing scenery in the dark. It was a twenty-minute drive back to her car, which she'd left in the Taney Motorsports parking lot. Determinedly, she said, "Let's talk about you and the team."

He sighed. "Can't we pull over and make out instead?"

Her traitorous body said *yes, please.* To her relief, her brain was still made of sterner stuff. "The team," she said firmly. "You can start by telling me how you got interested in NASCAR."

"That's not the team," he protested.

"Were your parents into racing?"

"My parents died when I was in college."

"How awful." Compassion stung behind Sandra's eyes. "What happened?"

"They were killed in a car accident on vacation in eastern Europe. Dad was in the diplomatic service, posted to Istanbul at the time. He and Mom always vacationed in the most exotic places."

"Did you and your brother live overseas with them?"

Taney shook his head. "Steve and I went to boarding schools here."

"Boarding school, is that where people started calling you 'Taney'?"

"Excuse me?"

"No one calls you Gideon," she said. "Not even your niece. It's weird."

He frowned. "I don't ask people not to use my first name—and Steve calls me Gideon."

"And you get on well with him, right?"

He examined her face for sarcasm. "I used to spend a lot of time with Steve and his wife, Lisa. They're huge NASCAR fans, and they got me interested. A few years later, I decided I wanted my own team."

His expression lit with remembered excitement. "That first year I set up Taney Motorsports, it was crazy. I had the worst driver in the field, I was my own biggest sponsor—I had to borrow from the bank to buy tires."

"I didn't realize you'd had any really bad years."

"It got a lot better after I fired the driver and hired Sam Garrett to replace him. I soon learned NASCAR is like any other business—you have to spend big to win big."

Sandra hoped that strategy would pay off soon in her own company. That the huge sum she'd borrowed to buy out her business partner would start garnering the exponential return she needed.

"The first couple of years were the best," he said. "I used to go see Steve and Lisa every Monday and we'd rehash race day. They didn't have a view on all the ins and outs, but it was good to get a fresh take on things."

"So what changed?" Sandra asked.

He shrugged. "One of the reasons I went in to NASCAR was because I wasn't getting as much satisfaction out of All Sports as I had when I first started. Then

NASCAR tailed off, too. I guess…I was looking for something I could get passionate about for the long term."

She smiled.

"What?"

"That's what you need to get back," she said. "That passion, that turn-on."

He looked away from the road long enough for his gaze to find her cleavage. "I'm turned on."

"I meant by…life."

His smile was one of exasperation. "It's not that simple, Sandra, believe me."

SANDRA'S HOPE of convincing Taney that NASCAR was a great place to be received a setback in Phoenix. A calamitous chain of events led to Will wrecking his car at practice. His crew chief, Seth Gallant, had the team setting up the alternate No. 467 car late into the night on Saturday, then early on Sunday. It was a night race, which relieved some of the pressure, but the guys were tired, tempers were frayed and the race seemed a disaster in the making.

Worse, because Will had wrecked right at the start of the practice, his feedback about the track and the accuracy of the setup was almost nonexistent. And even at the best of times driver feedback was a problem for the team. Seth had some strong views on the setup needed, based on watching other drivers, but the car chief, who was new to the team and had a great reputation, had been listening to the talk among his peers, and had a different view. Discussions that might have been rational under less pressure turned heated, then accusatory.

Sandra and Kylie arrived in the garage early on Sunday to make coffee and give moral support to the troops. Sandra had insisted Taney do the same. To her surprise, he'd agreed—but his set expression and cold eyes as he observed the chaos spoke louder than any shout of disapproval.

"Will you quit looking as if you're about to fire everyone?" she demanded as he helped her carry another round of coffees from the hauler to the garage. "You're making things worse."

"I seriously doubt they could be worse," he said.

She put her tray down on a stack of tires and folded her arms, knowing the movement highlighted her figure in her tight, scooped-neck T-shirt. Taney shot her a furious look that said, dammit, he didn't want to scope her out but now he was going to have to, and for half a second, he dropped his gaze. Then he was back, hazel eyes hot on hers.

"You know, Taney, I'm disappointed in you."

"Give it a rest," he growled. "When I want to know what you think, I'll ask you."

She raised her voice over the noise of the No. 467's engine. "You've built a reputation for being able to straighten out any mess, and as far as I can see, it's all hooey."

"Hooey?" Suddenly, he didn't look so annoyed.

She hadn't even realized she'd used that word. "It was one of my dad's favorite expressions, and sometimes it's the only one that fits."

His eyes rested on her mouth. "Did your dad die?"

"He— No, he just doesn't say hooey anymore. Stop trying to distract me, when you're the one person who can make this—" she waved a hand at the squabbling team "—better."

"I'm not a miracle worker."

"You're a born leader, according to you." She grabbed his upper arm with the intention of dragging him toward the team, but it was like wrapping her hands around a steel roll bar and trying to bend it.

He looked down at her hands on his arm, and shook his head. "What do you expect me to do?"

"What Jason Kemp should be doing but isn't, because he's scared one of the mechanics might throw a wrench at him. Make sure everyone knows who's in charge, and there's just one plan to fix it." She narrowed her eyes. "Or do you want Will's race to suck so badly that we lose Jack Carter?"

Taney's basketball buddy had called yesterday to say he wanted to talk numbers. They would meet with him after tonight's race. Sandra knew Taney wouldn't want to upset the deal by having Will drive badly.

Taney's long-suffering sigh told her he'd seen her point. He headed into the thick of the action.

"Guys, take a break, and let's find a different way to do this." It wasn't just his commanding voice and physical size that made people stand back and give him their attention, Sandra thought. It was that mysterious presence.

In half an hour, Taney had everyone doing what they should be, without griping. The tension in the garage had lowered considerably.

"Better?" He dusted his hands together as he and Sandra walked back out to the hauler.

"Much better. You did a great job." Taney looked better, too. There was a light in his eye that told her he'd enjoyed the challenge of getting the team under control.

ALYSSA RITCHIE picked her way through the garage, conscious that the eyes of almost every man were upon her.

It was hardly surprising, given the way a lot of the women dressed here. Alyssa's most glamorous competition was the NASCAR Sprint Cup Series cars.

Just because the garage dress code specified closed shoes and long pants, she didn't see any need to look like a slob. Nor like a sycophant—she couldn't believe the amount of driver-branded merchandise people wore, regardless of whether the cut, color or combination suited them. Her spiky-heeled red boots, black designer pants and crimson wrap top—a shade most blondes couldn't get away with—stood out. Given her new career, that was how it should be.

"Hello, Alyssa." MacKay Lundgren's lazy tone mocked her, his tall frame blocked her path, dwarfing her. The man had to be six-three or four, a height she considered completely unnecessary. "You have a nerve, showing up in enemy territory—do the Branches know you're here?" he asked.

"You again," she said icily, ignoring his question. She was unable to resist a quick glance around to see if anyone who mattered was nearby, in case MacKay planned another comment about her age. The fact that she was forty-five years old was between her and her birth certificate. To anyone else, she was late-thirties. In the publicity shots she'd had done for her recent tell-all book, she looked nearer thirty—they'd needed only the teeniest bit of air-brushing.

It turned out she and MacKay were alone in a pocket of space that right now no one else was invading. She didn't count the mechanic who couldn't hide his blatant admiration as he walked past. He was handsome and youthful enough to boost her ego, but definitely not earning in the right league.

"Any luck finding your new benefactor?" he asked.

She gave him a pitying smile. "Luck has nothing to do with it."

MacKay laughed, a rich, attractive sound. Alyssa guessed he was around her age—her real age—and the only lines on his face were laugh lines. Yet she didn't associate him with laughter; she always found him intense.

"What brings you here two weeks running?" she asked.

Those dark brown eyes were hooded. "Maybe it's you."

"Maybe it's not," she retorted. Though she didn't discount the intriguing possibility of MacKay having some complex pursuit in mind. But more likely, he was wheeling and dealing with someone in NASCAR. It might pay to keep an eye on him, because where MacKay went, money soon followed.

"I hear you've written a book," he said.

Alyssa raised her eyebrows. "If you've only just heard that you're behind the times. My little tell-all has been gathering headlines for a couple of months now, and it's not on the shelves until August."

Her book deal to write a scandalous tell-all about her life as mistress of America's most wanted white-collar criminal, along with her insights into the lives of the old-money, formerly ultra-rich Branch family and their cronies, had been front page headline news.

Speculation was rife as to what she would actually reveal.

"I don't read the tabloids," MacKay said. "Is it true you're producing a range of diet products, too?"

Now that wasn't in the newspapers. Yet. "Diet products first, then makeup, maybe fashion," she said. "All under my own brand—I'll be the next lifestyle guru."

"Martha Stewart for the wicked," he suggested.

She hid a smile. "Certainly my goal, like hers, is to help ordinary women. I've written a second book designed to show them how they can look like me."

His eyes wandered her curves. "You mean, like a directory of plastic surgeons?"

Once again, he almost annoyed her into betraying her trailer-trash roots by slapping him. But Hilton had taught her to wield words as weapons. "I've noticed," she said, "that some men resort to childish gibes when confronted by something they want but can't have."

He bared those thin lips in a grin that could only be called wolfish. "Sooner or later, I always get what I want."

MACKAY WATCHED Alyssa flounce away, and hoped that would prove true in this case. She was one hot woman.

She stopped to talk to Larry Preston, a team owner with more money than sense and therefore a likely target for her. The guy was practically drooling as Alyssa batted her eyelashes and gave him that little-girl-lost look that provided such a fascinating contrast with her vampish figure. She leaned into Preston, and he looked as if he was about to have a heart attack. Then she put her hand on his arm—MacKay remembered how her skin had felt last week, like very expensive silk. She looked as if she was asking a favor, and Preston was as eager to please as a puppy shown a bone.

MacKay had heard that Larry Preston was newly single. He wondered if Alyssa was looking for a more domestic arrangement—marriage—this time around. If Preston fell for her charms it would be his own stupid fault. One thing about Alyssa, she didn't try to hide what sort of person she was.

He shook his head. Why was he wasting time thinking about her, rather than pursing his NASCAR Sprint Cup Series sponsorship? He'd met Richard Latimer earlier, and Latimer had said he was in advanced discussions with another sponsor for Bart Branch, so it wasn't appropriate to talk to MacKay at the moment.

Will Branch needed a sponsor, too, but at this stage his team owner, Gideon Taney, was looking for more money than MacKay wanted to spend.

But he would have to find something soon—the auto finance business was due to launch in July.

MacKay took one last look at Alyssa, at her butt in those tight, tight pants, and quelled the pang of desire. He put her out of his mind, and went to work.

DESPITE DRIVING the backup car, Will didn't fare too badly. The team's belated effort to pull together, orchestrated by Taney, paid off and, helped by a handy pileup that took out three of the best drivers in the field, Will finished ninth.

It put everyone in a good mood—especially Taney, who was convinced Jack Carter would sign the deal to sponsor Will.

Of course, when he said that to Sandra she didn't agree. "There was something off about the guy," she said.

"That's just because he asked you to dinner."

She pffed. "Believe me, I want to like him. That raging attraction he has for me could come in handy when the new team owner wants to fire me. Jack might be the man to stand up for Motor Media Group."

Taney growled.

For privacy, they'd agreed to meet in his motor home,

which he'd brought out of storage now that he was making a habit of going to races again.

Taney handed out beers, and they clinked their bottles in a toast to Will's great run tonight.

Jack Carter leaned back against the leather couch and said, "Guys, I want to do a deal."

Taney couldn't help a sidelong, triumphant glance at Sandra. "That's great." This time next week, he'd have sold the team and be out of NASCAR for good.

"But not at the price we talked about."

Taney sipped his beer, looking relaxed. "The price we talked about is the price of the deal."

Jack laughed. "I'm assuming you're negotiable."

"Within reason."

"I can't pay more than four million this year," Jack said. "Five million next year, with an option for year three."

Taney heard Sandra's indrawn breath. He half expected her to blow a gasket. But it seemed she saved the worst of her temper for Taney—his privilege, he guessed—because she contented herself with an outbreak of tsking.

"That is not within reason," he pointed out mildly. "The numbers are too low, but more importantly we need a minimum three-year commitment."

"Which you won't get, not at this stage," Jack said, equally casually.

The conversation circled around in that vein for some time. By the end of it, they didn't have a deal, and it was obvious they weren't going to. Jack couldn't—or wouldn't—afford it.

After Jack left, Taney began tidying away so his driver could hit the road with the motor home and he and Sandra could head to the airport. He slanted Sandra a glance. "Anything you'd like to say to me?"

"I TOLD YOU SO."

"You did," he said seriously. "You have good instincts—I should have listened to you."

Sandra tried not to melt visibly. Did he know there was nothing sexier than a man who could admit to a woman he was wrong and, more importantly, she was right? "Be careful, you're bordering on sensitive," she warned him.

Too late, she realized what she was implying. Going by the knowing look that turned Taney's eyes almost green, so did he.

"Since my instincts are so good," she said hastily, "why not trust me when I tell you that selling Taney Motorsports won't make you happy?"

He bristled. "I'm happy."

"You'd be happier if you threw yourself into the team with some enthusiasm."

"Your instincts are good, but they're not that good."

"We're back to square one then," she said. "No sponsor, not even a hot prospect."

That peculiar wavelength that she and Taney shared quivered at the word *hot,* and he raised his eyebrows in unspoken question.

She shook her head, stifled a smile at his dramatic sigh of disappointment.

Taney wasn't a prospect for her personally. Not even if he changed his mind about selling the team. Quitter or no quitter, any guy whose motto was *Every man for himself* would never make the cut.

CHAPTER EIGHT

TANEY'S ADMISSION that he trusted her instincts was no use at all, Sandra realized as she dressed for work on Wednesday morning.

It hadn't influenced his decision to sell the team, and it made her feel guilty that she'd agreed to this morning's secret meeting in Charlotte with Mark Green's client.

It was a lose-lose situation.

She chose a powder-blue suit for the meeting, just in case the sponsor was willing to be impressed by womanly charms. The color heightened her femininity, and the cut was sharp and professional without hiding her curves.

By the time she'd finished her makeup, Sandra figured she'd only have a half hour in the office before the meeting, and even then she'd have to hurry. She rushed out the front door of her cottage in Concord, letting it bang behind her.

And ran right into Taney.

"Careful." He grasped her elbow as she teetered on the edge of the porch.

Darn it, they had one of those moments again, where his touch seeped right through to her core, where no matter how mad he'd made her, she ended up smiling, just because he was Taney and he was here.

He's the enemy.

"You look fantastic." *An enemy with a nice turn of phrase.* "That color really suits you." He hadn't let go of her elbow, and now his grip tightened.

Sandra pulled her simpering, pushover brain—the one responsible for the sappy smile she was pretty sure she was wearing—into line. She had to get out of here without alerting Taney to the fact that she was sneaking around behind his back.

"How did you know where I live?" she said discouragingly, her tone sufficiently at odds with her smile for him to look puzzled.

"Your home address is on your business card." He held up the incriminating piece of card. "Which isn't a good idea," he reproved. "You need to keep your business and personal lives separate."

"*You're* the one who keeps saying you want to kiss me," she said, outraged. Then she realized from the enjoyment in his eyes that he was joking.

"I thought you'd never ask," he said with relief, and wrapped his arms around her. The man was incorrigible.

Sandra reminded herself the sense of safety within his embrace was an illusion. "I didn't ask for this." She thumped his chest.

"Ouch." He caught her hand, held it in place over his heart. "You don't know your own strength," he chided.

It seemed to Sandra that they were frozen in place, the spring day on pause around them, save for the tiniest breeze that caressed her skin.

Taney shook his head as if to clear it. "Now, about that kiss." His fingers moved at her waist, massaging, stroking. Sandra squirmed. "Where should I start?" he mused. He edged closer so her hips were snug against his; her insides turned liquid. "Hmm, maybe with your lips." He cocked his head to one side. "Maybe that delicious ear. Or maybe…" His gaze dropped lower.

"Oh, for Pete's sake, just kiss me," she said, in an agony of wanting.

She didn't miss the supreme satisfaction that curved his mouth right before he touched it to hers.

She didn't care, she just needed to be in his arms, tasting him, matching his kisses with her own. She broke off long enough to say, "This is only a kiss, I still don't date quitters," then abandoned herself to the exploration of his tongue, his mouth. He made a noise against her that might have been a chuckle, then showed her who was boss by making "just a kiss" last until he was ready to stop.

By the time he relinquished his hold on her, Sandra's blouse had come untucked and the powder-blue suit jacket had been unceremoniously pushed down her arms to land on the porch. She staggered slightly as she stepped away from him.

"Why are you here? I assume it wasn't just for that kiss." Mindful she didn't have much time before her meeting, Sandra began the process of restoring her appearance.

He watched her retuck her blouse, then almost unconsciously reached to help her. The brush of his fingers against her abdomen made her want to start all over again. "We need to talk about where we go next with our sponsors—I thought we could do it over breakfast," he said.

She knew where *she* was going next—to a meeting she hadn't told him about. Her cheeks warmed, and she hurriedly bent to pick up her jacket.

Taney swooped to grab her keys, which must have fallen out of a pocket. Instead of handing them to her, he strode to the door and unlocked it.

"Taney, I'm going out."

He pushed the door open. "I'm so used to eating with you, I don't know how to go solo anymore."

It was a joke, but Sandra knew what he meant. They'd had so many meals together it had started to feel…right.

"What happened to, 'every man for himself'?" she said lightly.

He started, as if he hadn't realized he'd contradicted his much-vaunted creed of independence. He gave her a brooding look, rubbed his chin. "Interesting question. Come inside and we'll discuss it."

"Hey, this is *my* house and I've already had breakfast." She was addressing his broad, uncompromising back—he'd already crossed the threshold of her territory and was by some male feeding instinct headed unerringly for the kitchen.

She followed him. "I can't do breakfast, I have a…an appointment with my personal trainer." To reinforce the lie, she added, "I haven't been for so long, the calories are growing on my hips like barnacles."

He'd reached his destination, and now he made a leisurely inspection of her hips—and several other curves as well—that had her heating up all over again. "Cancel it," he said persuasively. "I've never seen anyone less in need of shaping up."

Really? She pushed away the flattered feeling. "Rico gets annoyed if I cancel."

"Rico's your trainer?"

"Uh-huh." Some devil prompted her to add, "He's very sensitive."

Taney folded his arms, his body language telling her he refused to be drawn by her provocation. Instead, he scanned the kitchen, taking in the weathered pine cabinetry, the old marble counter that was cracked in places but still beautiful, the flourishes of color where she'd painted the joinery a sky blue.

"Nice place," he said. "Cozy. You're quite the home-maker."

"When I have time." She sighed. "Which I don't right now. Taney, I have to leave."

He picked up the low-fat yogurt container she'd left on the counter. "Was this breakfast?" he said, disgusted.

"I had two plums with it. Very nutritious." She grabbed the container and threw it in the trash.

"I can see I'm going to have to use my secret weapon." He reached into the pocket of his sports jacket and pulled out…a Krispy Kreme bag.

Sandra groaned.

He opened the bag and waved it under her nose. "Lemon-filled or blueberry?"

"Blueberry," she said automatically. Because, curse her weakness, the blueberry came with powdered sugar on top, while the lemon had only a glaze.

He held it to her lips and she took a bite. "Mmm."

"Mmm," he agreed, watching her mouth.

Sandra grabbed the donut from him. "I have to go. Let's talk tomorrow on the flight to Talladega." She'd taken to traveling to the races on Taney's plane rather than the team aircraft.

"I'm flying out early for a meeting with the guy who wants to buy the team," he said.

She flinched and—although it wasn't easy around a

mouthful of donut—managed to say coldly, "Then I'll have to try and pin you down at some stage over the weekend."

"Really?" he said hopefully.

He was impossible. Most of the time he was way too stern and serious, and just when things were getting important, he turned into a joker. She pointed a finger at the doorway. "Out. Now."

At last he left, and Sandra hurried to her car. As she drove, she pulled out her cell phone. She'd make an appointment with Rico for tonight, so the story she'd told Taney wouldn't be a total lie.

SHE REACHED the attorney's office ten minutes late, so she took the elevator to the third floor, even though her hips could have done with the walk.

Mark Green emerged in response to the receptionist's call. He shook Sandra's hand and cast an appreciative eye over her appearance. "My client is already here. Come into my office and I'll introduce you."

From the doorway, Sandra saw a slim, elegantly clad frame and a mane of bleached-blond hair. The mystery sponsor was a woman. She turned around, and although Sandra had never met her, no introduction was needed.

Sandra's first instinct was to walk out. But she was getting desperate.

"Alyssa Ritchie," she said flatly.

Alyssa's perfectly shaped eyebrows rose in surprised pleasure at her notoriety. "And you must be Sandra Jacobs."

She extended a hand, and her fine-boned fingers with their scarlet nails made Sandra feel like a giant. Alyssa was tall, though several inches shorter than Sandra, but she was also reed-slim, as if she'd whipped every ounce of fat into submission. That slimness highlighted the impressiveness of her cleavage, peeking out from a camisole beneath her cropped jacket. Her natural assets had been augmented by a prominent plastic surgeon, according to a "friend" of Alyssa's who'd told all to a national newspaper.

Alyssa had to be several years older than Sandra, given she'd been Hilton Branch's mistress for twenty years—but everything about her was sexy, from the sheer panty hose that gleamed on her legs beneath her short, short skirt, to the diamond pendant nestling in her cleavage, to that care-lessly perfect blond hair.

Alyssa's body had won her fame—or infamy—and a reported fortune.

Her career as the mistress of Hilton Branch, Will and Bart's father, had been a secret right up until Hilton's dis-appearance with the bank's money. Alyssa had cashed in on the media frenzy by announcing to the world that she was Hilton's lover. The revelation had devastated the Branches—and launched Alyssa into the headlines, where she managed to stay by drip-feeding gossip about Hilton and other lovers who'd enjoyed her charms.

Alyssa's request to meet with Sandra could only mean trouble.

The blonde bombshell looked amused, as if she'd read Sandra's mind. "I should start by telling you my interest in sponsoring Will Branch is genuine." She sat down, waited for Sandra to do the same. The attorney excused himself.

Sandra perched on the edge of her seat. "You do know the sponsorship is worth many millions of dollars?"

"Money is not a problem." Alyssa's assured, discreet tone grated, given how indiscreet she was about her relationships.

"You can't be planning to promote your book through NASCAR sponsorship," Sandra said doubtfully.

Alyssa smiled condescendingly. "I'm looking to promote *Slim Like Me,* my new healthy living book and range of diet products. My backers are very confident— they're prepared to invest heavily."

"I've never heard of it."

"Exactly." Alyssa crossed one leg over the other. "The line launches in August, simultaneously with my autobiography." A fancy name for an exposé, Sandra thought. "NASCAR has a tremendous female fan base and the media opportunities are substantial. I want a slim, good-looking driver to promote the *Slim Like Me* brand."

"There are lots of slim, good-looking NASCAR drivers," Sandra said. "You don't have to choose your lover's son."

Alyssa laughed. "After what Will said about Olivia Winton, I assure you he's the perfect candidate. That gaffe polarized women. They either love him or hate him. But—" she shrugged "—lots of women hate me, too. That doesn't mean they don't want to look like me—it doesn't mean they won't pick up my book just so they can despise me all over again. And it doesn't mean they don't want to be attractive to a handsome young driver."

She tossed her head, and her hair landed exactly where it had been before. How did she do that?

"The link between me and Will, through Hilton, will attract plenty of media attention," Alyssa said. "And that's money in the bank for *Slim Like Me.*"

Alyssa was willing to court controversy all the way, Sandra saw. The woman was right. Having people hate you was almost as good as having people love you; the kiss of death was lukewarmness.

"Even if you're able to make us a generous offer, I'm sure you're not so naive as to expect a warm welcome from Taney Motorsports," Sandra said.

"I don't expect Will to welcome me," Alyssa corrected her. "But it's not his decision."

"You obviously have doubts about Gideon Taney," Sandra pointed out, "or you would have invited him to this meeting." A horrible thought struck her. "Taney's not mentioned in your book, is he?"

Alyssa somehow managed to convey a frown without getting a single line in her brow. "Gideon Taney is far too dull to make it into my book. But he's a good friend of Maeve Branch." Maeve was Hilton's wife. "I want your advice so I can get my offer into a shape that'll be hard for Taney to turn down on loyalty grounds."

How ironic that a cynic like Alyssa was probably over-estimating Taney's loyalty. Sandra suspected his friendship with Maeve wouldn't stop him signing with Alyssa. *Every man for himself* didn't take account of friendship.

She almost wished she shared his view. If Alyssa had her heart set on Will, why not take her money and secure Motor Media Group's cash flow? If only Sandra could overlook that Will would hate—and probably refuse—to promote his father's mistress's business, and that Bart—her other main client—and the rest of the family would be hurt, too. If only she could ignore the sleazy origin of Alyssa's money, and convince herself that Will's job was to drive the car, and Sandra's was to promote him and his sponsors in whatever way she could.

"I've read the proposal you sent my attorney," Alyssa said, businesslike now. "The dollars are too high. And you're too desperate to hold out for that kind of money. I want to understand from you what value I'll get in terms of publicity. I'll use that to calculate a sum I can offer Taney."

Sandra reluctantly relinquished the fantasy in which she was as hardhearted as Taney and Alyssa. She stood. "I can't support you as a sponsor for Will. It would hurt him."

Alyssa made a disbelieving noise.

"Your involvement would also hurt Will's driving and that'll hurt the whole team." It was another good reason to turn the woman down, one that even Taney would have to consider. "I know Taney feels the same," she lied. "If you really want to sponsor a team, I'm sure you'll find another opportunity."

Alyssa's mouth tightened. "There are other opportunities, but this one has the most media potential. I know it'll be a winner for me."

"It won't," Sandra said, "because you can't have it."

As she left, she thought about how Taney would have reacted in this morning's meeting. Chances were he'd have taken the money. He wouldn't be around to handle the fallout. That would be left to her or her replacement.

Sandra made her decision as to what she would tell Taney about Alyssa's interest.

Nothing.

SANDRA'S CELL PHONE rang as she checked in to her hotel in Pell City, near the track at Talladega.

"I'm glad you're here." It was Bart Branch. The twins had flown in earlier on another driver's plane. "Will's in trouble."

"What now?" Sandra handed over her reservation confirmation to the clerk.

"He met a girl."

Sandra groaned.

"He's in her hotel room and her boyfriend's waiting outside the door with his buddies. His *big* buddies."

"Could your brother be any stupider?" Sandra took the card key the clerk handed over. In an instant change of plan, she asked the clerk to store her bag. "Tell me where you are," she said to Bart as she walked briskly outside. It was still sunny, but the early-evening chill had set in. She got into the first of the two cabs waiting outside the hotel.

Bart gave her the details. "I'm in the lobby," he said, "and, uh, so are a bunch of reporters. They haven't seen me yet, but one of the boyfriend's buddies must have called them because they're asking for Will."

Sandra repeated the address to the cab driver, then said to Bart, "Tell them you're Will and keep them talking."

There was a silence. Then an admiring, "Not bad."

It wasn't far to the hotel where Will was trysting. Sandra used the journey to think fast about how she would handle the situation, including the "big buddies."

Taney. His name popped into her head. He was bound to be bigger than the guys waiting to pounce on Will, and even if he wasn't, he exuded authority. If anyone could get rid of this problem without either the police or the press finding out, it would be Taney.

She dialed his cell. Four rings, then voice mail. Dammit, this was so typical! He would have seen her incoming call and decided he didn't want her hassling him, or that he had more important things to do. In a tight, tense voice, she left a message. She wouldn't hold her breath that he would get it—she was on her own. Just for a change.

At the hotel—one of those no-frills chain places that attracts travelers who don't want to move too far off the interstate—Sandra walked through the lobby with only the briefest of glances at Bart, who was still chatting with the reporters. He met her gaze long enough to convey that nothing had changed, so Sandra took the elevator to the third floor.

She didn't need the room number Bart had given her. There was only one door with a bunch of beefy, angry young men outside. Sandra told herself she was taller than most of them, and started down the corridor.

One of the men thumped a fist on the door and yelled, "When are you going to come out, Branch?"

The threat led to a chorus of "Yeah" and "When?" and "C'mon, sissy-boy" from his associates.

Thank goodness the media hadn't found their way up here. But all it would take would be the Brawn Brothers deciding to knock the door down, which they looked mad enough to do, and they'd be on the six o'clock news.

Sandra's pace slowed as she neared the men. Maybe this was a dumb idea, going in alone.

One of the men began tapping experimentally around the hotel room door, as if he was trying to gauge the best place to apply a shoulder. His actions meant Sandra didn't have a choice. She cleared her throat and said in her lowest, most commanding voice, "Hey, guys, is Will Branch around?"

There was a moment's silence while they processed her arrival.

The man who'd thumped on the door offered a truculent, "None of your damned business."

"It is my business," she said pleasantly. "I'm Will's…

boss. That's my driver you're haranguing, and I can't allow it."

There was an outburst of angry explanations, punctuated by threats to dismember Will. The gist of it was, as Bart had said, that Will was in the room with Thumper's girlfriend, and had, unreasonably in the men's view, refused all requests to open the door and allow himself to be torn apart.

Sandra decided she might just tear him apart herself when this was over.

A couple of the guys had their eyes pinned to her bosom—hooray for tight-fitting, deep *V* T-shirts—so it wasn't too hard to push her way through. She knocked on the door. "Will?"

"Sandra, is that you?" Unmistakable relief in her driver's voice.

"What's going on? The truth."

"I got chatting to Lacey at a bar nearby—she's a big fan."

They always were.

"We were talking, that's all," Will said. "Then her boyfriend showed up and got abusive, calling her a slut, so Lacey dumped him."

"Serves you right," Sandra told the red-faced Thumper.

"He got mad, looked as if he might hit her. Lacey was scared, so I told her I'd see her back to her hotel. But butt-face out there—"

"No name-calling," Sandra said sharply, in case someone decided to take their hurt feelings out on her.

"He followed us."

"I want to speak to Lacey," Sandra said.

There was a murmured consultation between Will and the

girl, who agreed to talk to Sandra. She confirmed Will's story.

How ironic, Sandra thought. For once, Will had behaved in a manner worthy of his Southern gentleman's upbringing, and it had all gone wrong.

CHAPTER NINE

TANEY STEPPED OUT of the elevator and was alarmed to see Sandra surrounded by a half-dozen guys who looked as if they'd had a few drinks and were frisky on it.

The surge of protectiveness that flooded him took his breath away.

Why hadn't she waited for him to get here? She must have known he wouldn't want her marching into a situation like this. When one of the men put a hand on her arm, Taney bared his teeth in a silent snarl and hoped the guy had said his last prayers. He was about to show the lowlife just what a mistake he'd made, when Sandra snapped, "Hands off, bucko, or you'll be answering to my six-foot-four gorilla boyfriend."

Taney's snarl dissolved into a proud grin. *That's my girl.* Then he clicked. *Six foot four?* Check. *Gorilla?* She would pay for that.

The guy obeyed, and in an impressively authoritative voice, Sandra said to the one who appeared to be the luckless guy whose girl had run off with Will, "You've got the wrong idea. There's nothing going on between Will and Lacey."

"Then why won't he come out?" the guy demanded.

Sensing that the immediate threat of violence had faded, Taney stepped into the ice machine alcove. If Sandra could handle it, he should let her.

"Because your goons—" Sandra waved an exasperated hand at his cronies "—plan to hurt him. And he has to drive in the race on Sunday."

The men went into a huddle to plan their next move. When they emerged, the boyfriend said, "Okay, we won't hurt him. But he has to come out now and promise he won't see Lacey again."

This was deteriorating into the kind of dating farce Taney hadn't witnessed since high school.

Sandra told Will the conditions for his safe exit, and he agreed with alacrity.

"You need to leave Lacey alone, too," she told the boyfriend. He eventually agreed, but Sandra couldn't convince him to walk away before he was certain Will had left.

From the alcove, Taney could see Sandra sweating as if she was brokering a Middle East peace deal in the desert. Not because of the physical threat, he guessed, but because of the implications for Will and their sponsor hunt. Will's reputation wouldn't survive another incident so soon after the Olivia Winton disaster.

She pushed damp tendrils of hair off her face—Taney had to resist the urge to go and help her with that—and blew out a cooling breath.

Somehow she managed to marshal the guys in a line against the wall on the other side of the corridor—very impressive. Sandra stood in the middle and called, "You can come out, Will."

The hotel room door opened, just a crack.

"Come out, sissy-boy," jeered the boyfriend. When Sandra's glare hit him, he shut up.

Taney cheered her silently.

Will came out of the room, somewhat sheepishly. "I would have fought those guys, but I knew you wouldn't want me to get in any more trouble."

"Darned right," she approved. "Let's go."

All would have been fine and dandy, if Lacey hadn't stuck her head around the door and said breathlessly, adoringly, "Thanks, Will, I'll never forget you."

With a roar of rage, the boyfriend launched himself off the wall. Sandra—the brave, gorgeous, crazy *idiot*—put herself between him and Will. To his credit, Will elbowed her aside and rushed to meet his man.

But that gesture would undo all of Sandra's brilliant diplomacy.

Taney made his move. "Hey." He stepped out of the alcove and the surprise factor got everyone's attention.

SANDRA BIT DOWN on a shriek, because they didn't need any more hysteria around here. When had Taney arrived?

The dynamic in the hallway changed, instantly and dramatically. The good guys—Sandra and Will—were suddenly magnified by the large, controlled and inspiring presence of Taney. The bad guys looked smaller, insignificant, no matter that there were more of them. Thumper lowered his fist and took a step away from Will, who managed to arrest the momentum that was about to propel his shoulder into the guy's chest.

Nothing about Taney was aggressive or intimidating, but in five seconds he'd achieved more than Sandra had in a hot, sweaty and sometimes fear-filled fifteen minutes.

"Are you okay?" Taney said.

"I am now."

He turned a dark gaze on Will.

"None of this was Will's fault," she said quickly. "He was playing the Good Samaritan and doing a good job of it."

Taney nodded. "Will, could you go downstairs and rescue your brother from the media hordes in the lobby? Head back to your motor home, and I'll see you there."

Will made himself scarce, and this time, although Lacey had stepped out of the room, she didn't say anything that would set her boyfriend off. Taney turned to the boyfriend. "If you'll promise me there'll be no more trouble, I'll ask our NASCAR Nationwide Series sponsor to offer you and your pals some of their guest tickets for tomorrow's race. You'll even get to eat their free food and beer." He crossed his fingers that the sponsor, with whom he had an excellent relationship, would have tickets available and would cooperate.

The guys all but salivated at the thought of having access to the garage. It was a great idea of Taney's, Sandra thought. Will wouldn't be at Saturday's race, so the goons wouldn't bother him.

"Where are you staying?" Taney asked the boyfriend. "I'll have the passes sent to you."

The guy reddened, waved his hand at Lacey's door.

Taney's mouth flattened. "Not anymore, you're not." He turned to the goons. "Any of you have room for this guy?"

One of them put up his hand, as if he was in school and Taney was the principal.

"You have two minutes to collect your gear from in there." Taney nodded toward the room. Lacey's boyfriend didn't argue. He was back out a minute and a half later, carrying a blue duffel with clothes spilling out.

"You can go in now," Taney told Lacey. It was an order, and she obeyed.

"Off you go." Taney dismissed the men, getting room details from one so he could send up their passes.

Just like that, the drama was over. The corridor was empty, except for Taney and Sandra. Sandra's knees sagged; Taney slung an arm around her shoulders. "Hang in there, sweetheart."

Sweetheart?

"I'm okay." But she leaned in to him a little. "When did you get here?"

"About the time you managed to convince the boyfriend nothing was going on."

"You might have said something sooner," she said, indignant. "It could have turned nasty any moment."

"When it did, I stepped in."

"I suppose I should be grateful," she said tartly, "that you didn't decide it was *every man for himself* and walk away."

Taney frowned. "Up until Lacey made that stupid parting comment, you had the situation under control. You were outstanding. I was awestruck."

"Humph," she said.

His grip tightened on her shoulder. "I was here when you needed me," he reminded her with soft intensity.

The words resounded within her, imbued with far more significance than he could have intended.

"You didn't answer your phone when I called," she countered weakly. She moved away from him before she did something dumb like burst into overwrought tears.

"I just missed your call. I checked your message right away and came straight here. I guess I should have called to say I was coming."

"You should've," she agreed.

Maybe it was a reaction to the stress, or maybe it was the way Taney was looking at her, but she felt a strange, clenching tension around her heart.

He dusted her cheek with a knuckle. "Feisty little thing, aren't you?"

Now her heart felt as if it was swelling behind her ribs. "No one," she said slowly, "has ever called me that."

His mouth quirked in disbelief. "They might not have said feisty, but I'm sure you've heard assertive, gutsy, plucky, brave…"

"Little," she said. "No one has ever called me little."

"Oh. Huh." He looked her up and down, and a speculative light came into his eyes. "Obviously you're not short."

"Obviously," she agreed.

"You're not fine-boned."

"Careful," she warned.

He chuckled. "You're smarter and stronger than any woman I know."

She knew she was smart and strong, but having Taney say it made her feel invincible.

"But sometimes, and I'm warning you—" he took her hands loosely in his "—to a woman who wants a sensitive guy, this might come across as way too macho…."

"I think I can handle it."

"Of course you can, because you're smart and strong." His clasp tightened on her fingers as if to hold her in place. "Sometimes, to me, you seem little."

Sandra absorbed the strength of the fingers curled around hers.

"Are you going to slug me?" he asked.

"Not this time." For the first time in her life she felt too petite and delicate to slug anything bigger than a gnat.

"Have dinner with me tonight." It was a demand, not an invitation.

She blinked. "Where did that come from?"

"You don't want a sensitive guy any more than I want to wear a tutu."

She smiled at the image. "I've always thought pink might be your color."

"I want us to go on a date. A real date."

"I told you I don't date—"

"I'm your boyfriend." He narrowed his eyes. "Your *six-foot-four gorilla.*"

She clapped a hand to her mouth. "That was poetic license. I wasn't talking about you, I was just using you as a reference point for my imagination."

He pressed a kiss to her forehead. "I use you as a reference point for my imagination, too."

She felt herself blush. "Don't you have a sponsor dinner lined up for tonight?"

His mouth flattened. "We've run out of prospects." For the first time, he looked disheartened. "If I don't have a sponsor by the time we get to the Charlotte race next month, my buyer's going to look elsewhere. We've got to find someone."

This was Sandra's opportunity to mention Alyssa Ritchie. But after today's troubles, she didn't want that woman intruding on her evening with Taney. "So, dinner tonight," she said.

"You don't have to call it a date if you don't want to." Taney patted her shoulder reassuringly. "Call it, 'We both have to eat.'"

"What are you going to call it?"

"Oh, I'm definitely calling it a date."

Was it a date if only one of them said it was? Sandra thought not.

"I'm the boss," he reminded her. "If I say you have to come to dinner, you have to."

That gave her an idea. "Let's make it a business dinner. That meeting we need to have."

"Nope. We're not going to discuss work at all."

She frowned. "What will we talk about? You're not very good at opening up."

The look he gave her was very patient, yet somehow implied he was reaching the end of his tether. "Whatever people talk about when they're on a date. Mutual friends, parties they've been to, music, books."

"*I* can talk about that," she said doubtfully. "But whether you can…"

He narrowed his eyes. "I promise," he said softly, "you'll find me fascinating."

The low timbre of his voice sent a shiver through her. She wanted to go on a date with him, so badly it hurt. *I deserve it,* she told herself. She remembered that he'd had a meeting today with the man who planned to buy Taney Motorsports. Soon, Taney wouldn't even be her client. So there was no harm in one date.

She started to shiver as perspiration cooled on her skin. Taney chafed her arms with his large, warm hands. "You sure you're okay?"

"I just need a shower. And a change of clothes. And a—"

Her cell phone rang and she pulled it out of her pocket. She groaned, and answered the call.

"Dr. Zakursky, I meant to let you know I was going out of town, but I, uh, forgot…." She listened to a short lecture from the doctor about the value of his time, then ended the call.

"Didn't you go to the doctor just last week?" Taney asked.

"Didn't I tell you it's none of your business just last week?" She gave him a sunny smile and let him take her elbow as they headed to the elevator. "Uh, Taney, what should I wear to dinner?"

He slanted her a grin. "Don't go soft on me now, Sandra. Wear whatever makes you feel good."

Sidelong, she met his gaze, saw the danger lurking.

"My nun's habit," she said decisively.

Taney gave a shout of laughter. "I'll pick you up at your hotel at seven, Sister."

CHAPTER TEN

As a P.R. CONSULTANT, Sandra always traveled prepared for unexpected social occasions. The black strappy dress she'd packed for Talladega would take her anywhere from a barbecue to, in a pinch, a ball. Or to dinner with Taney.

She was quite satisfied with her appearance when she looked in the mirror. And going by the flare of green heat in Taney's eyes, he was happy, too, though all he said was a mild, "Looks like that whole nun thing has changed since I last went to church."

Then he took her arm with a firmness that spoke of possession.

Sandra couldn't identify any other NASCAR people at the restaurant Taney had chosen. But then, teams and drivers didn't usually veer to the candlelit-table, leather-bound-menu end of the restaurant scale.

Taney sat back, entirely relaxed in the plush surroundings. His eyes ran over her face, her shoulders, lingered on her cleavage. He smiled. And her skin burned as if he'd reached across and touched her.

The waiter served bread, took their orders, then poured the champagne Taney had requested.

Sandra eased back into her seat and marveled that she felt so relaxed with him—and not just because of the champagne bubbles working their way gently into her bloodstream. A few weeks ago she'd been always on edge in his presence. The edge hadn't gone away, but it felt…different.

It feels way too good.

Which didn't make sense, because, outside of work, she and Taney were almost strangers. If Danielle hadn't run away from home, Sandra still wouldn't know he had a brother, or that his parents had died. The man opposite her was an uncharted continent of history, opinions, thoughts and emotions. She wanted to explore.

Of course, she hadn't told him much about herself, but that was because she didn't want him to figure out her business was in trouble. Taney hadn't asked about her family, she realized. It would have been logical when they'd discussed his background, but he hadn't said a word.

Maybe he's not interested. The thought alarmed her, alerted her to the fact that she felt more for him than she'd admitted to herself. Surely it couldn't all be one-sided?

"Taney," she said, "since this is our first date, is there anything you'd like to know about me?"

He scrutinized her face, a half smile on his lips. "As a matter of fact, there is."

He is interested, she told herself, relieved. *He just hasn't had a chance to ask.*

He leaned forward across the table, caught her hand in his. "I can't stop wondering," he said, "what you look like naked."

Sandra gave a little squawk of shock and tried to tug her hand back. But he held fast.

"I think I have a pretty good picture," he reflected, "but I can't be sure."

Her whole body was one giant blush. "That's not

what I meant," she chided. "I meant about my family, my background."

He shrugged. "Why don't you tell me about your parents?"

He didn't sound as if he really wanted to know, and alarm pricked Sandra. She wanted to know what made Taney tick. Why didn't he feel the same?

"Mom and Dad live at Sunny Hills, a retirement complex near Kannapolis," she said. Although he hadn't asked, she added, "I'm an only child."

If he asked about her folks' ages, or their health, she would tell him about her father's Alzheimer's, her fears for the future, that her parents' financial dependence was choking her. She longed to share that with someone strong like Taney. Someone who might care for her.

"Were they involved in NASCAR?"

It was a frustratingly superficial question. She tugged her hand free from his on the pretext of adjusting her napkin. "Only as fans. Dad had a tool-making business." She put a toe in the water of personal revelation and said, "His company went broke when I was in college."

"Ouch. That's too bad." No questions about how or why. What was wrong with him? Sandra laced her fingers on the table, and waded in up to her knees. "One of the staff took advantage of some bad decisions Dad made. He watched the company slide downhill, then when it hit the bottom he bought the business for a song."

She sat back while the waiter set her scallops in dill cream sauce in front of her. It smelled delicious, delicately herby, richly creamy. But Sandra was losing her appetite. Still, she sampled a scallop while Taney took a spoonful of his seafood chowder.

"It was MacKay Lundgren," she said.

Taney suspended his spoon between plate and mouth, at last taking an interest. "Lundgren worked for your dad?"

She nodded. "Right out of college. You could say my father started him on his brilliant career of taking advantage of others."

"Did Lundgren do anything illegal?" Taney asked.

"I...don't think so." That wasn't the point. "Mom and Dad lost everything."

"That must have been tough." He sounded sympathetic, yet she felt he wasn't that involved in the conversation. To her consternation, tears started in her eyes.

"Sandra?" He reached for her hand again, squeezed her fingers. "Are you okay, sweetheart?" The endearment, spoken for the second time today, went some way toward reassuring her.

She wiped her eyes with her free hand. "I know a lot of people admire Lundgren for his ability to make something out of nothing, but I'm not one of them. He really hurt my family."

"I'm sorry," he said, and this time he sounded as if he meant it. He lifted her hand to his lips, kissed her knuckles.

Her scallops seemed more appetizing and she concentrated on eating her meal. Men weren't as interested in the intimate details of people's lives as women were, she reminded herself.

That was why she had a hundred and one questions for Taney, and he had none for her. Apart from that naked one. She smiled to herself and added the same question about him to her list. A hundred and two questions.

Their entrées arrived—Angus beef for Taney, venison for Sandra. The waiter went through the ritual of grinding black pepper over their plates and pouring the glasses of red wine Taney had ordered to accompany their rich meals.

"What's the most serious relationship you've ever had?" she asked Taney. She might as well start working her way down the list. "I mean, with a woman. How long did it last?"

"That would be my marriage."

Sandra's fork clattered on to her plate. "You've been *married?*"

He set his own cutlery down. "It was a long time ago."

"You're divorced?" She imagined the failure that implied wouldn't sit well with him.

He shook his head. "My wife died—we'd only been married a year."

"Taney, I'm so sorry." She tried to picture a younger, more vulnerable Taney and found she hated the thought of him hurting, grieving.

"Tess and I tied the knot right out of college. She'd just started teaching elementary school—I was starting up All Sports. We probably should have waited, but she wanted to get married."

"And you didn't?" She concentrated on slicing through her perfectly medium-rare venison.

He waited until she'd finished, until his silence brought her gaze to his. He said deliberately, "The marriage meant more to her than it did to me. But she knew I was a different kind of person from her, it didn't worry her that I was less…engaged."

Sandra had the sense he'd compiled this explanation out of the death of his marriage and yet he wasn't sure it was the right one.

"It sounds a little odd," she said carefully, "to say you were married but you weren't engaged."

"That's the semantics," he said. "Put it this way, I loved Tess and if she was still alive, we'd still be together. It's just, marriage wasn't the key to my happiness."

"What was?" Sandra asked.

He looked surprised. "I…don't know."

"How did Tess die?"

"She went on a teaching sabbatical to Central America," Taney said. "She wanted me to go along, but I couldn't take time out from the business. Soon after she arrived, she caught a virus. They were a long way from a hospital—she died before they got there."

He picked up his red wine and swirled the glass in front of him, studying the contents intently. But he didn't drink.

"You feel guilty," Sandra guessed from that intense concentration.

He lifted his gaze. "Not about Tess dying. Even if I'd been there, I couldn't have stopped that virus killing her. If I feel any guilt, it's because I didn't love her as much as I should have, as much as she wanted me to. I think, if we'd had longer, that love would have grown."

To Sandra, it didn't sound like much of a plan. Warning bells clanged in her head. Nothing she'd learned on her first date with Taney made him the kind of guy she wanted.

And yet, still, she wanted him.

She dredged a piece of venison through the juniper berry sauce and brought it up to her mouth. The aroma of spices tantalized her, tempted her to abandon this complex minefield of a conversation and just enjoy her meal.

But if she didn't ask questions now, she might be in too deep by the time she found out she didn't like the answers.

"What you said about not being engaged in your marriage…"

A shadow of annoyance crossed his face. "That probably wasn't the right word. It's not relevant now, anyway."

"I think it is the right word, and it is relevant," Sandra said. "I think you have trouble engaging with other people in meaningful, sharing relationships."

He stared at her, then his face darkened. "Since when are you my shrink? And since when is this the kind of conversation you have on a first date?"

"If you think this is our first date, you're deluding yourself."

"You said it wasn't a date at all," he protested.

"Lately you've *engaged* with me more than you have with anyone else, as far as I can see. You've kissed me—several times—and you never mentioned you were married."

"It's not something you say to a woman right before you kiss her," he growled.

"Would you ever have told me, if I hadn't asked?"

"Of course," he snapped.

"Your life is full of unfinished or incomplete relationships," she said. "You had years at boarding school, your parents died, then your wife…have you ever had a lasting, intimate relationship where you've had to dig inside and share your deepest self?"

He recoiled. "I have lots of strong relationships."

"You've never asked me about my past or my family, you don't return your brother's calls, you used me as a buffer between you and your niece." Sandra reeled with the realization of just how empty Taney's relationships were. "You stay away from the one thing you've been passionate about in recent years—NASCAR—and you've made *every man for himself* some kind of gold standard for survival." She spread her hands to say *I rest my case.*

TANEY'S HEART thudded at the injustice of Sandra's judgment. Sure, if you took each of her points, there was something in what she'd said. But they weren't the sum of him.

"First up—" he began to check off his arguments on his fingers "—I loved my wife, and you can't take that away. Second, my brother and I are very close and just because I don't know what to say to a thirteen-year-old girl that doesn't mean we don't have a relationship." His voice was getting louder, but he was so damned mad, he didn't care. "And it's naive to think one thing—one passion—can satisfy you all your life, so selling the team is a natural progression. And lastly—" He stopped.

"Lastly what?"

Damn, he'd forgotten. Sandra had folded her arms, pushing up her curves in that slinky black dress. Taney didn't want to prove to her how emotionally engaged he was—what the hell did that mean anyway, and why had he come up with such a stupid word? He stood, and two strides took him to her side of the table, right up close. Sandra tipped her head back to see him.

"Lastly, *this.*" He cupped the back of her head with his hand, then he bent down, lowered his mouth to hers for a swift, hard kiss. It was over too quickly, and he came back for another one, longer, exulting in her instant response.

When he released her, her cheeks were hot and flushed. But her voice was cold. "What exactly did that prove?"

"Nothing, I just felt like doing it." Taney returned to his

seat and said sarcastically, "Because I'm an emotionally outgoing guy."

Impervious to the sarcasm she said, "Exactly what *emotion* were you exhibiting there?"

Taney firmed his jaw. "Lust."

"Lust is not an emotion."

She would know, of course, because she knew everything.

"Maybe I just have a wider emotional repertoire than you."

"You're an emotional infant, Taney," she snapped. "Even if it's not all your own fault."

"Well, thank you very much."

"You keep all your relationships skin-deep. Doesn't it tell you something that you think lust is an emotion?" Her eyes sparked blue heat. "You've never allowed yourself to be tested, to see whether you can stick at a relationship, and as a result, you can't even handle the easy problems, like Danielle running away. You've never learned to engage in a way that'll keep you there through thick and thin."

"You have no idea what you're talking about." Taney was too enraged to yell; the words came out almost a whisper.

"I think I do." Her face was tense, set, anxious, but her chin lifted high.

He couldn't believe this date had gone so wrong. Sandra looked incredible tonight. Strong and sexy. He'd already realized the more time he spent with her, the more he wanted her. And not just for a night, or a week or a month. He had a feeling he could spend a long time with her.

And now she was telling him he was, what, an *emo-*

tional infant? There was no response he could make to that, feeling as angry as he did, that wouldn't prove her point.

Which meant she'd won this battle.

But Taney wanted her and he would have her.

He would win the war.

CHAPTER ELEVEN

As Taney walked from his motor home to the garage in Talladega, he felt happier than he had in a long time.

He shouldn't have, because he was furious with Sandra. Added to which, there were no sponsorship prospects in sight for Will. If he didn't find one soon, his buyer would get sick of waiting.

But it was hard to get upset about that with the sun shining and the smell of engine oil and gas, barbecue and hot pavement vying for sensory appreciation.

Besides, this thing with Sandra…it wasn't as if he didn't know what to do about it. She'd gotten the wrong end of the stick, judged his relationships on what she'd seen at work and on some apparent failure on his part to ask her about her parents. For Pete's sake, if she'd said she wanted him to ask, he'd have done it in a heartbeat. Excuse him for not having ESP. No, he knew for sure, she was wrong about this "engagement" stuff, and all he had to do was show her. And he knew just how to do it.

He didn't know where their relationship was going, but it was in the right direction, and he planned to enjoy the journey. Doubtless she wouldn't make it easy—half the fun of being with her was the way she insisted on challenging him—but he was prepared to work at it. Which was something, even Sandra would have to agree.

He knew she had three top-flight media interviews arranged for Will this morning, so about the time she was due to finish, he headed for the media center. He waited a minute while she bid farewell to the journalists—the interview had gone well, going by the smiles all around—then approached her.

"There's someone I want you to meet." He made his voice friendly, casual, and he could see she was relieved.

They'd parted on cool terms last night—arctic terms—having both said things they shouldn't. He wanted to put that behind them, and he was betting she would, too. She darted him a tentative smile, and she looked so damned beautiful, something caught in his throat. She didn't argue, didn't say anything, just fell in beside him. As they headed for the garage, Taney's arm brushed hers. Just that whisper of sensation sent his thoughts careening on ahead to their next date, to the next time he kissed her, to when he would make love to her.

It'd better be soon, or this was going to play havoc with his concentration.

He led her to the Taney Motorsports garage, toward the family clustered a considerate distance from the car and the team whose setup job was done, but who couldn't leave the car alone, as if their constant checks and handling would keep the No. 467 primed and dangerous.

"There's Danielle," Sandra said, surprised.

"Yep." He grabbed her hand, not worried that people would see, and took her to meet his family. "Guys, I'd like you to meet Sandra Jacobs. Sandra, this is my brother, Steve, and his wife, Lisa. You've met Danielle, and this little troublemaker is Josh."

He ruffled the hair of his ten-year-old nephew, whose

startled flinch suggested physical affection from Taney wasn't a regular occurrence—which didn't mean he wasn't fully engaged with his family.

"So," he joked to Danielle, "been on any escapades lately?" She rewarded him with a scowl. Oh, yeah, he'd forgotten to talk to her dad about the quarter midget.

He moved on quickly to Steve and Lisa. Annoyingly, their eyes popped out of their heads at the sight of Taney holding Sandra's hand. It had been a long time since he'd introduced them to a date. But that didn't mean he didn't have serious relationships.

SANDRA FIGURED Taney had a point to prove after the way she'd taken him down last night. She'd gone too far, probably. But the words had poured out of her—what she'd discovered about him had been so surprising, she couldn't keep quiet.

If he wanted to prove her wrong, good for him. She hoped he could. But she wouldn't hold her breath.

Maybe it was a positive sign that Steve and Lisa were so likable and obviously well-adjusted. Steve looked similar to Taney, but was of a leaner build, not so broad across the shoulders. Lisa was much shorter than her husband, and maybe because of that he seemed very protective toward her. He treated her like a princess, but thankfully she had no airs and graces.

"Do you have time to join us for our picnic?" Lisa asked Sandra.

"I'm not sure." Presumably the fact that Taney was holding her hand meant he wanted her to join them; she slid him a querying glance.

"Of course you do," Taney said. He grinned, looking

surprisingly lighthearted after last night. "I'm the boss, and I say you have time."

She rolled her eyes.

As they set up the tailgate picnic, Steve Taney kept up a running commentary on how much things cost: the rental car, the beers he'd bought on special, the preprepared salads from the deli, the radio scanner he'd hired at the speedway entrance so he could listen to the in-car conversations.

It seemed an odd preoccupation, when judging by their clothes and watches, the family was comfortably wealthy. Lisa caught Sandra's bemusement.

"Steve's an accountant," she explained. "He actually has no objection to spending money, but he finds prices fascinating. As you can imagine, I never let him come with me to the supermarket—it's too embarrassing—and I can't let him go on his own because he's there for three hours."

Her husband dropped a kiss on her nose. "Thanks, sweetheart, you make me sound like such a fun guy."

She wrapped her arms around him and kissed him full on the mouth. "You were a lot of fun this morning, honey."

"Too much information," Taney protested.

But Steve was looking so pleased with himself, and Lisa so content, that Sandra couldn't help envying them.

Despite the fact that the food was all store-bought, with the exception of a carrot cake Lisa had brought with her on the plane, the picnic was tasty.

Danielle appeared to be in a snit with her uncle and her parents—she spoke when spoken to, but that was all. However, she went out of her way to be friendly toward Sandra, which amused the other adults.

Sandra found herself getting the third degree from

Steve. He asked about Motor Media Group—his wife slapped his arm when he asked what Sandra's turnover was and how much profit she'd made last year. From there, he moved on to her family, and Sandra found herself repeating the information she'd given Taney last night.

"How much does your parents' retirement facility set them back?" Steve asked. His brother showed more interest than Taney had, Sandra thought ruefully.

She told him the annual payments. Steve whistled.

"It's a very good place," she assured him.

Taney looked sharply at her. "Who pays the fees, if your parents were broke?"

Now he was full of questions. She pressed her lips together. "I do." Some of the men she'd dated had been horrified at how much she spent on her parents' care.

Taney nodded. "Good."

She shrugged. "They're my parents."

The sun had moved around enough that it was getting in her eyes. She pulled her sunglasses out of her purse and put them on.

"Nice shades," Lisa said.

Sandra saw Steve open his mouth. "A hundred and eighty bucks," she said, and everyone laughed.

TANEY STOOD and extended a hand to Sandra to pull her up. "We need to get back to the garage."

Steve shook his hand in an oddly formal farewell. "'Bye, Taney."

Taney walked back to the garage alongside Sandra. The picnic had gone well, mostly. But he wasn't sure how far he'd advanced his cause. It wasn't lost on him that his brother had instinctively asked Sandra all the questions about her parents that she'd wanted Taney to. It wasn't until he was almost at the garage that Taney realized Steve had called him Taney, rather than Gideon. How long had his brother been doing that?

In the garage, Will was conferring with Seth Gallant.

"Guys, I need a word," Taney said. At Sandra's urging, he'd started to make a habit of having a quick chat to the two men ahead of the race, understanding the strategy they'd agreed upon, learning what the main areas of concern were for that day's event. Sandra felt it made the guys think harder about what they were doing and why. She might even be right.

Today, though, Taney skipped the technicalities and launched into a pep talk.

"When you're in that car out there, Will, I don't want you thinking black and white."

Will squinted against the glare of the sun streaming in through the garage opening. "You don't want me thinking about the checkered flag too early?"

Taney laughed. Sometimes, Will was an idiot. But then the lead-up to a race was pretty stressful. "What I'm saying is, there's a whole bunch of people out there who know for sure you're not going to win today."

Will looked startled at Taney's bluntness; Seth made a sound of protest.

"But NASCAR is just like life," Taney said. "People think they know, but they're just guessing. The only thing that's black and white is what's already happened. The future is gray—none of us can say for sure what'll happen on that track today." He put a hand on Will's shoulder. "I believe you have it in you to win, Will, I wouldn't have hired you otherwise."

He applied pressure with that hand. "I don't want you to go out there today looking backward, letting the black and white, what you know about your racing so far this season, affect how you drive today. You don't know how you're going to do—neither do I. Get out there, do your damnedest."

TANEY WATCHED the race with Sandra in the pits. Will had qualified fourteenth, which wasn't bad.

At the fall of the green flag, every driver out there was ready to fight for pavement on NASCAR's longest and fastest track.

Will's performance fluctuated in the opening laps. He passed a couple of cars, then fell back again. But after about lap twenty, he seemed to hit his stride and managed to hold his own against the superfast competition.

Half the battle at Talladega was staying out of trouble when the excitement got to be too much and drivers started crashing into each other. With the help of his spotter, Will managed to avoid two pileups that sucked other drivers in.

After the third pit stop, he was running with the lead pack in the single file draft that characterized the superspeedway races. If Will was going to get farther ahead, he'd have to team up with another driver so they could use the improved airflow over two cars to allow a pass.

Taney found himself wondering who would pull out first. If it was Will, he'd need the support of another driver or he'd be stranded high and dry, that most pathetic of objects—a single car on a superspeedway track.

It took a long time, but at last Will made his move. Justin Murphy pulled out behind him, giving both drivers the aerodynamics they needed to maintain a passing speed.

Soon, Will was in fourth, Murphy fifth. Then a collective gasp rose from the crowd.

"Did you see that?" Sandra grabbed Taney's arm. "Justin Murphy nudged Will."

He grinned down at her, amused at the outrage in her face. "I saw."

"We ought to complain," she said.

"It was just your standard nudge."

"It was a *lot* harder than your standard nudge."

"Was not." It was, actually, but Taney would rather argue with her.

"Was, too." She *nudged* him, hard in the ribs.

"Hey." He went for her ribs with his fingers, tickling until she squealed for mercy.

He released her suddenly as, six laps from the end, Will passed front-runner Kent Grosso in a notoriously difficult slingshot move, bringing the crowd to its feet. Taney cheered as hard as anyone else.

"He's in the lead," Sandra screamed.

Taney put a hand over his ear. "You don't say." But her excitement was infectious, and he hauled her close and kissed her. "I didn't know Will could drive like that."

"Like you said, no one knows what he's capable of until he does it."

"So I did." Taney grinned. He was pretty sure his pep talk had made the difference today, and going by the way Sandra was hanging on to his arm and squeezing whenever Will did something right, she knew it, too.

But Grosso wasn't about to take Will's pass without a fight. On the last lap, the crowd gasped when it became apparent Grosso was attempting a slingshot move of his own.

He didn't manage to pull it off. He misjudged the clearance to pull out behind Will. Grosso hit the No. 467 car's back bumper.

As Will's car smashed, spun, then smashed again, Grosso sailed past the checkered flag to victory.

"No!" Sandra groaned. She looked as if she was about to cry.

Taney loved that she got so steamed up about things. "That's NASCAR, sweetheart." He found he wasn't upset; Will had driven so well, it was a triumph in itself. "You can be right up front, then in an instant you're out of the race."

"You say that as if it's a good thing," she protested.

"It's a great thing." He grabbed her wrist, put a finger to her pulse, felt it thudding. "Look how excited you are."

She laughed, admitting it.

Taney felt exactly the same. This was what Sandra had been telling him he ought to feel. And he did.

PHYSICALLY, Will was fine after the accident—but he was mighty peeved that Kent Grosso had robbed him of his first win. He was in demand from the media, who wanted to know the reason for his sudden improved performance.

Will wasn't giving any secrets away, but his eyes met Taney's across the crowd of reporters.

"I was proud of you today, Will." Taney's praise, given later in the garage, went some way toward making up for the disappointment, Sandra could see. "You keep that up, and we'll have a Cup contender on our hands."

"Yes, sir." Will was uncharacteristically respectful, not at all arrogant as he'd been known to be on the rare occasions he'd raced well.

Taney's pep talk about not letting the past ruin the present had obviously struck a chord with Will. As it had with Sandra. She wondered if Taney had been trying to tell *her* something, too. That she shouldn't judge his ability to enter into a relationship with her by what he'd done in the past.

Will's face darkened.

Sandra turned—and saw Alyssa Ritchie, tripping along in the stupidest pair of boots she'd ever seen in a garage. *Oh, no.*

She should have told Taney about Alyssa's offer—right now, she couldn't imagine why she'd been so stupid. Was there any chance Alyssa wasn't here to cause trouble?

Alyssa's eyes met hers, cool and determined. "Sandra, we meet again."

Sandra felt both Taney's and Will's eyes boring into her. This couldn't end well.

Unless she could bluff her way out of it.

Then, later, she'd tell Taney all about it—silently she promised him, promised herself, promised the world she would confess—if only, right now, Alyssa would go away without revealing Sandra's deception.

"Hey, Alyssa, how are you?" She injected the warmth of long acquaintance into her voice. Maybe they'd believe she and Alyssa went way back. "You look amazing."

Alyssa was so surprised—Sandra figured she didn't receive many compliments from women—that there was a moment of inaction, in which Sandra could begin shepherding her out of the Taney Motorsports garage area. "We're busy packing up, but how about I call you tomorrow?"

She got six paces before Alyssa dug her spiky red heels in. "I want to talk—" she put her hands on her hips, which had the effect of thrusting out her chest "—now."

"Please, Alyssa—" Dammit, she'd given the game away. No matter that Sandra's smile didn't slip, she'd let a pleading note into her voice that showed how badly she didn't want this encounter. Alyssa's eyebrows rose, then a playful—in a cat-and-mouse way—smile curved her lips. She strutted toward Will and Taney, leaving Sandra counting down to disaster.

"Too bad you crashed," Alyssa said to Will. "You'll be lucky to find sponsorship from anyone other than an auto wrecker."

Sandra figured it was only NASCAR's media training with regard to cursing that kept Will's lips clamped together.

"You'd better leave," Taney said.

Alyssa cocked a hip in sultry defiance. "I figure after today's fiasco you might be desperate enough to accept my offer, no matter what Sandra says about your loyalties."

Sandra gulped, and closed her eyes. When she opened them again, Taney was looking right at her. Puzzled. Doubting. Then, when she tried to transmit a mute apology, his face set in hard lines.

"We're far from desperate," he told Alyssa. "We've been caught up in talks with several parties, which is why we haven't got back to you sooner."

That was how you bluffed, Sandra thought. None of this pathetic be-my-pal stuff.

"But I'll call you personally tomorrow," he said to Alyssa. His gaze flicked dismissively past Sandra. But the vibes shooting in her direction said, *You are so dead, lady.*

"That's more like it," Alyssa purred.

"No way," Will blurted. "*She* doesn't get to be my sponsor." He interspersed his objection with a number of curses. Sandra groaned inwardly when she noticed a reporter pricking up his ears at Will's choice of language—and the NASCAR official right beside him.

Taney quelled Will with a look and said to Alyssa, "But for now, we have a garage to pack up. As I said, you'd better leave."

Sandra didn't realize she was holding her breath until Alyssa walked away.

Taney spent a couple of minutes in discussion with the NASCAR official about Will's language infringement. Sandra hoped the time would allow the anger she saw in the rigid length of his spine, and the unforgiving set of his chin, to diminish. Even a little.

CHAPTER TWELVE

FOR ONCE, Alyssa saw MacKay before he saw her. It gave her time to make a choice. Dawdle behind him in the parking lot until he'd climbed into his car, or talk to the man.

Normally, she'd have stayed clear of him. But now that her bid for Will Branch's sponsorship looked as if it might go ahead, she could use the advice of someone savvy.

There weren't many people she trusted and were willing to ask. Most thought they were better than her, or wanted her to fail.

She didn't think MacKay felt any such malevolence toward her, but did she trust him? There was nothing inherently trustworthy about him. But like her, he was a NASCAR outsider, and he would have no reason to betray her confidence to those on the inside.

She'd subconsciously quickened her pace, so already she was gaining on him. As if he'd sensed he was the target of her thoughts, Lundgren turned. Even from ten feet away, she caught the appreciation in his intense brown eyes as he surveyed her short, fitted jacket buttoned over a lacy camisole and diamanté-studded jeans. She sashayed over to him.

"Alyssa, you're all-out fascinated by cars these days," he said.

She laid a hand on his arm and cooed, "They're so big and powerful."

His eyes narrowed. "And there are so many rich men around."

"You're one of them." She allowed rare approval into her tone.

"Perhaps I should have said, there are so many rich fools. It's an important distinction."

Lundgren was no fool, which he proved when she moistened her lips with her tongue, then bit her lip in a way she knew made her look adorably vulnerable. At least, it had ten years ago. He merely rolled his eyes and said, "What do you want?"

Fine by her, she preferred the direct approach, too. "I need your advice on a business deal I'm considering."

He folded his arms, looked down his long nose at her. "I'm busy."

She ignored that statement. "Thanks to my generous backers, I can invest heavily to promote my slimming products. I'm looking at a sponsorship opportunity, and the numbers are complicated."

He said abruptly, "Where's your car?"

"Over there." She pointed the way.

"I'll walk you to it while you tell me more, and I'll see if I'm interested in helping you."

He matched his long legs to her slower pace as they headed for her BMW convertible, hidden from view by the trucks and SUVs that dominated the parking lot.

"I'm considering sponsoring Will Branch in the NASCAR Sprint Cup Series, but I'm not sure how to assess the value so that I can set my bid at the right level. I'd like to run a few figures past you, see if you think they're realistic."

"Will Branch? That's nervy." He shook his head, disbelieving. "But you don't need me. You have an accountant for that kind of thing."

"I need someone with marketing flair," she said. "Someone with guts."

"Guts." They'd reached her car, and he leaned against it. "*You'll* need guts if you plan to sponsor Hilton's son—you'll be the most hated woman in NASCAR."

"I already am," she said impatiently. "Just tell me if you'll look at the numbers."

"Yes," he said.

She hadn't expected such easy acquiescence—Lundgren was no Boy Scout. "Why would you do that?"

He looked at her and his eyes darkened. "Why do you think?"

He stepped closer to her and all at once her insides quivered like a bow drawn tight. He was a handsome man—not in the pinup sense, but with a worldly charm that seduced her. Perhaps the most fascinating thing about him, she thought, was the contrast between his lazy eyes and the ruthless line of his mouth.

Alyssa stood her ground, tilted her face up to his. The spark between them was so hot, she felt her cheeks heat in a way they hadn't since she was…well, not in a long time.

But she wasn't going to make the first move. She looked him in the eye, challenged him to kiss her. If she had to pay a price for his help, it was up to him to exact it. And he wouldn't get as much as he wanted.

For a long moment, he stared back. Then he shook his head slowly, once, twice.

Surely he wasn't about to walk away. He wanted her too much.

But maybe that shake of the head was just frustration at his own unwelcome interest in her, because a second later his hands clamped around Alyssa's arms, locking her in place, and his mouth came down on hers.

No gentle preamble, no hesitation that might be construed as checking he had permission to kiss her. MacKay went straight in for the kill, his lips hard and hungry. And with just one touch, Alyssa was on fire.

She didn't waste time pretending she didn't want this. She kissed him back, at first frantically, trying to get all she could of him in case he ended it. But then it became obvious he was just as caught up as she was. His arms went around her, pulling her to him.

Alyssa shifted against him, reveled in his groan of longing and explored his mouth with unfamiliar fervor.

He pushed her against her car, and the hunger eased into something gentler, something infinitely more unsettling. Alyssa pulled away, mortified to find she was panting.

MacKay's cheeks were darkened, his eyes hot. But when he said, "Not bad," it was with the refined air Hilton had adopted whenever he sampled a top-notch claret but didn't want to overexcite the wine waiter.

Alyssa slowed her breathing. "Adequate," she agreed. She reached into her purse for her business card. "Call me in the next couple of days, let me know when we can meet."

He pocketed the card, sauntered away without another word. Leaving Alyssa wondering who had won.

TANEY DIDN'T MIND supporting Will in the discussion about his cursing with the NASCAR official. He was almost willing to prolong it if it meant postponing dealing with Sandra. He couldn't remember being so angry.

What galled him most was that his anger was intermingled with hurt and with his feelings for Sandra. That hurt, those feelings, wouldn't let his anger be the pure and simple response it should be.

From the way her eyes widened in alarm when he walked back to her, he gathered she saw only the anger. *Good.* Taney wasn't about to let her anxiety tug at his heart.

He grabbed her elbow, frog-marched her out of the garage and into the hauler. Seth was in the office, writing up his notes on the race. He took one look at Taney's face and cleared out.

"Taney, I can explain." It was the first thing Sandra had said since Alyssa had revealed her duplicity.

Too late.

He pushed her down onto the squab that provided seating for the built-in table.

"Alyssa asked me to meet with her in confidence last week," Sandra said. "The call came through her lawyer— I didn't know it was her. I agreed, assuming the next step would be to get you involved."

"But you didn't do that." He didn't give her a chance to defend herself. "What did she want?"

"She's launching a range of slimming products, she thinks a NASCAR sponsorship will help. Taney, that woman is nothing but bad news."

"Any sponsorship offer is *good* news," he snapped.

"She's dragging the sordid details of her relationship with Will's father through the media. Think how he'll feel."

That's what she was worried about? How immature, brattish Will Branch would feel? What about how Taney felt about the woman he…liked…a lot…lying to him and sneaking behind his back?

She continued, "Having Alyssa Ritchie's slimming product on our car—"

"On *my* car!" he shouted. "I told you last night I need a sponsor before Charlotte. By not mentioning Alyssa you were sabotaging the sale of the team."

She paled. "I wasn't."

His fists curled on the table in frustration. "You've accused me of being secretive, of not sharing. What do you call this?"

"Alyssa seemed such a bad idea…."

"And you didn't trust me to judge that?" he demanded.

"No, I didn't," she burst out. "You just said, any offer is a good offer. Don't you care that Alyssa's making a fortune out of hurting other people?"

"I don't scrutinize the private lives of anyone I do business with at All Sports," he said. "Taney Motorsports is business, too."

"So it's every man for himself," she said witheringly. "If you sign with Alyssa, Will's going to drive badly and that'll demoralize the team."

"Drivers can be fired," he said. "And the team's future performance will be the concern of the new owner."

"You are such a—"

"You lied to me," he roared. "You called me on not being honest and open and not *engaging* with people." As much as he was angry with her, he was angry with himself for taking this so personally. "If you were anyone else, I'd fire you."

Of course, it was a threat that never cowed her, never produced the humility that might have salved his wrath. Her chin went up. "So why don't you? Maybe it's because you know I'm right."

Maybe it was because he would miss her.

He looked at her, and suddenly it wasn't business—it was all personal.

"You're a hypocrite," he said. "You're asking me for something you're not willing to give."

TANEY WAS STILL MAD with Sandra by the time of their regular Monday morning review meeting, for which she was late, of course. Amazing that she was always on time for media interviews, but the woman had no idea how to be punctual for anything else.

With legs like hers she should be a fast walker, she should get everywhere on time. She sat down in the chair next to Taney's, and he caught a glimpse of smooth thigh as her skirt rode up. He could do with seeing less of that, too. He didn't want to be reminded of how gorgeous she was. His overly personal reaction to her deception told him he was already in deeper than he wanted to be.

"I spoke to Alyssa this morning," he said. "She's coming in on Thursday to discuss the opportunity. She's talking a bid of five million for the rest of this season."

"That's nowhere near enough." She shrugged off her jacket, perhaps heated by indignation.

As usual, she wore a V-necked blouse that offered a glimpse of her stunning curves. It seemed to him she dressed to flaunt her assets. If it hadn't been so damned distracting, he would have applauded it.

"It would be five million more than we have now," he said crankily. "I don't know what she's offering the next two years, but we'll want at least seven mil for each."

Her lips pursed. "And to think Alyssa was worried your friendship with Hilton's wife might work against her."

"It's not a five-million-dollar friendship," he said, telling it like it was. "You might not like Alyssa, but she's all we've got." He noticed Sandra seemed paler than usual. Maybe, like him, she hadn't slept well. "Unless you have any other bright ideas?"

She cupped her chin in her hands, drawing Taney's attention to her mouth. "If you're willing to consider offers at the five-million level, I suggest we spread the news far and wide. That should smoke out a few more prospects. Then, if we end up with a couple of deals on the table, we might be able to get an auction going."

"That's probably about all we can do," he agreed.

Sandra suggested they set a deadline—the day after the race at Darlington—by which interested sponsors had to submit their offers.

From now on, there would be nothing subtle about their campaign. As Alyssa had pointed out, they were desperate.

MACKAY HAD THREE GOALS in mind when he turned up at Alyssa's condo in Charlotte for their meeting at nine o'clock on Tuesday night.

One: good old-fashioned industrial espionage.

Two: don't kiss her again.

Three: kiss her again.

Clearly, one of those goals was doomed to failure. He wasn't certain which.

He couldn't believe the way he'd responded to Alyssa's practiced charms like a sixteen-year-old out of his depth on his first date. He'd planned to kiss her just enough to convince her that attraction was behind his generous offer of help.

It had taken all of two seconds for control to fly out the window. He'd known kissing her would be good—he hadn't known it would be fantastic. Hence his dilemma tonight. He had to choose between a repeat of that incredible experience, or being certain he was in control. He sighed. At least the espionage would be uncomplicated.

Alyssa kept him waiting plenty long before she responded to his buzz on her doorbell. She opened the door wearing a mandarin-collared white silk dress that hugged her curves down to her thighs, then loosened off courtesy of a slit designed to allow ease of movement, but also to give a very tempting view of her legs.

MacKay followed her into the open-plan kitchen and living area, and found that it, too, was white—walls, carpet, ceilings, even most of the furniture.

"I'll apologize in advance in case I step on you," he told her. "I just might not see you."

It wasn't that funny, but for once her smile seemed genuine as she directed him to sit on one of the white chairs at the dining table—glass, so it might as well be white—where she had spread out some papers.

"Would you like a glass of wine?" A particularly fine Sonoma chardonnay stood on the table, along with two glasses.

"Sure." Because his throat was going dry just looking at her.

She'd piled her hair on top of her head, maybe with the idea of looking businesslike, but the blond mass appeared to be held in place by a collection of loose pins that implied the whole lot would come tumbling down if he tugged on one. Her lipstick was a bold raspberry color that made him want to taste her and her eyes looked wider, bluer, thanks to the use of who-knew-what artifice.

"I didn't know you had a condo here in Charlotte," he said.

"This is Hilton's." She poured the wine. "Mine's in Fort Worth."

"I thought all Hilton's assets were seized by the investigators."

She lifted her glass in a toast. "They don't know about this one and neither do the Branches. The ownership is in the name of a trust. I'll keep using it until they find it."

He took a sip of the perfectly chilled wine. "You don't feel guilty about depriving Hilton's poor wife and children?"

"I doubt Hilton's poor wife and children would see a penny of any proceeds that came from selling this place," she retorted. "Besides, I deserve it."

His gaze flicked over her. "You earned it."

"How about we get to work?" Her voice cooled. "I don't want to keep you."

He didn't believe that for one minute.

They got started, and MacKay, in the guise of helping her, was able to glean exactly the information he needed. There was even an added bonus when Alyssa said, "Taney announced yesterday that they're opening up the sponsorship to bids five million and above."

"Is anyone bidding against you?"

"Not that I know of. But Taney is very discreet." Thoughtful, she tapped her pen on the page in front of her. "Why are you helping me, MacKay?"

"Would you believe, because I like you?"

"That wouldn't be a good enough reason. It worries me that I don't know what you want."

"I want you."

"I told you that you can't have me, yet you're still here."

"I'm confident."

His assertion produced a small smile. A sudden twinge of guilt propelled MacKay out of his chair. He crossed the room to check out a small but stunning abstract canvas.

"It's a Beatrice Kane," she said.

"I know. She's very good." It was like describing that kiss they'd shared as very good. The painting was brilliant.

MacKay made up his mind about which of his goals he would fail on. He walked back to the table, held out his hand. Alyssa held his gaze. Then she stood, put her hand in his and walked with him to the white suede couch. Still standing, he drew her into his arms.

Once again, the kiss was cataclysmic. He couldn't stay on his feet, he had to push her down onto the couch so he could lie with her, run his hands over her stunning curves as he explored her mouth. Alyssa arched against him, entwined her arms around his neck and responded to his kiss with a compulsive fervor. She moved against him, sinuous and sensuous.

MacKay had no idea how long they lay there. Alyssa worked his shirt off him and her hands tortured him as she caressed his back, his chest. But he soon discovered there was no way her clothes were coming off. Every time his hand tried to explore, she slapped him away with a warning that he wasn't entitled.

She was driving him nuts.

At last, he could take it no more, and he had to stop, or die of frustration. Exhausted, he lay there, Alyssa in his arms, and closed his eyes.

He woke to find a pot of coffee and two mugs on the

glass coffee table. Hell, he'd fallen into a post-sex snooze, and he hadn't even had the sex! He must be getting old.

Alyssa, her white dress crumpled and her hair tumbling around her head—those pins had been a lot more effective than he'd predicted, but he'd gotten them out in the end—poured the coffee while MacKay put on his shirt. She took her mug and sat on the armchair that matched the couch. It seemed strange to use the term *restful* in conjunction with a siren like Alyssa, yet right now, he felt at ease.

"Do you miss Hilton?"

"I'm furious with him. He always said if he ever went away he'd take me with him." She sipped her coffee. "I assumed he meant if he left Maeve, not if he skipped the country with a stolen fortune."

"You were with him a long time."

She crossed one leg over the other, and that slit fell open. "When I first met Hilton, he fell in love with me, and I fell in love with his money. He said he would leave Maeve, I'd just need to wait a few months." She shook her head at her own naiveté. "Of course, that never happened. Three years later I'd fallen in love with him, he'd fallen out of love with me but was still very much in lust, and Maeve was there to stay."

"You were in love?" he said skeptically. "From what I know of Hilton, he's a selfish jerk—what's to love?" The money, he assumed.

"Hilton was good to me when no one else had been." She fixed a challenging gaze on MacKay. "Other men had used me, and hadn't bothered to take care of me the way he did. Hilton's brand of caring was seductive."

MacKay found he was disturbed at the thought of men

taking advantage of her—though he didn't doubt she'd exploited their interest to the full. "But you're not still in love with him?"

She shook her head. "I loved him for twelve years—longer than a lot of marriages last. About five years ago I woke up and realized he meant nothing to me beyond a friendship."

"You could have left then." MacKay calculated he'd been in marriage number three at the time.

She shrugged. "By that time I was a little old to be offering myself on the open market. Hilton was still good to me, fond of me in his own cheating way."

"He cheated on you?"

"Of course." She raised a cynical eyebrow. "A man who cheats on his wife is going to cheat on his mistress—wouldn't you say?"

MacKay laughed. "You're asking the wrong guy. I was a faithful husband."

"Not." It was obvious she didn't for one second entertain that he might be telling the truth. "How many wives have you had?"

"Just three."

She laughed. "And you were faithful to them all?"

"I get rid of them rather than cheat on them." He swigged his coffee. "It helps me maintain an illusion of integrity." He put his cup down, and stood. "I'll wash my hands, then I'll go."

ALYSSA LEANED BACK into the cushions, suddenly tired. What a strange evening. MacKay had been helpful beyond her imagining. He'd been good company, too, chatting with her as they worked—about things that assumed she had a brain in her head, not just inconsequentials. And that session on the couch… *Disturbing* was the only word that fit.

She'd worn this modest—for her—dress purely to annoy the hell out of MacKay, who would obviously prefer to see a lot more flesh. But it had turned into a tool for seduction…on both sides. Keeping her clothes on had proved strangely exciting, and she'd only just been able to remind herself not to hand him anything on a plate.

The encounter had left her dissatisfied. She'd wanted to drive him wild with desire and with regret that he couldn't have her, but had almost ended up out of control herself.

His cell phone vibrated on the table in front of her; she picked it up. The display read *Mom*.

MacKay Lundgren had a mother he liked enough to keep her number stored in his phone? She'd picked him as a runaway or an orphan, he had such a hungry look about him.

Before she thought better of it, Alyssa pressed the answer button.

"Mac, it's me." His mother's voice was youthful. Sharp, but also warm.

"MacKay is busy just now," Alyssa said.

"Who are you?" She didn't seem fazed to hear a strange woman answer her son's phone at—Alyssa glanced at her watch—past midnight. Alyssa detected only interest in the question.

"Alyssa," she said noncommittally.

"I'm Bettina," the woman said. "Are you Mac's girl-friend?"

Alyssa didn't get on well with women, so she never

bothered to sugarcoat her words to her own sex. "No, I'm too good for him."

A crack of laughter came down the line. "Did he say that?"

Alyssa stood and began to smooth the creases out of her dress. "We don't talk much—I'm a 36D cup." They'd done plenty of talking tonight, but that was the exception.

"That's always been his weakness," Bettina said resignedly. What an odd conversation to be having with MacKay's mother. "Can you tell him I'm expecting him for dinner next week, he just has to call and tell me what day."

"I suppose so."

"You can come, too, if you like," Bettina said.

About to turn her down with a blunt comment about the million things she'd rather do than spend an evening with MacKay and his mother, it dawned on Alyssa that if there was one way to infuriate the man, it would be to pretend she wanted to meet his mom. Men—even the sleaziest— saw their mothers as sacrosanct, and never introduced women like Alyssa to them.

"In that case," she said, "let's make it Tuesday."

She felt a lot better about facing MacKay when he returned from the bathroom. She'd already blotted out the memory of the broad firmness of his naked torso, and now managed to ignore that he looked rumpled and sexy, and softer than he had earlier.

The kiss he planted on her mouth wasn't soft. It was possessive and arrogant—she could tell he assumed from tonight's peculiar intimacy that she was available for more.

With pleasure, she held out his phone. "Your mom called, we're having dinner at her place next Tuesday night."

"We?" Predictably, he grabbed the phone as if she'd contaminated it. He scanned the received calls list to check she was telling the truth. "What did you say to my mother?"

"That I'd love to come to dinner. Oh, and that you like my body."

He groaned.

"You can't deny it," she said acidly. "You've had your hands all over me tonight." The urgent explorations of those hands would have had her begging for more if she hadn't had phenomenal willpower.

"Forget dinner," he said flatly. "You're not going anywhere near my mother."

He was right, of course. She had no intention of going to dinner. "She sounds delightful and I can't wait to meet her." She stalked to the front door, held it open for him. "See you Tuesday."

CHAPTER THIRTEEN

WORD GOT AROUND fast about the lower price tag on Will Branch's sponsorship, and by the end of the week Taney had received several phone calls. One of them was from MacKay Lundgren.

When Lundgren gave his name, Taney's first thought was a recollection of the quiver in Sandra's mouth when she'd mentioned Lundgren's involvement in her parents' business.

His second thought was of the way she'd concealed Alyssa's interest from him. He sat back and listened to what Lundgren had to say.

"I'm looking for a NASCAR opportunity to promote the new auto finance division of Lundgren Group," MacKay said.

"And we finally got down to your level?"

Lundgren didn't take offense at Taney's dig about his notoriously penny-pinching attitude to business. "Put it this way," he said. "I'll pay you more than Alyssa Ritchie's offering."

Taney sat straighter; Lundgren was up with the play, and it sounded as if he was serious.

"I suspect you—and your driver—will find me a more palatable business partner than Ms. Ritchie," Lundgren continued.

"You're not exactly squeaky clean," Taney pointed out.

"That wouldn't be your publicist talking, would it?"

"I understand you took advantage of her father."

Lundgren whistled through his teeth. "I worked for Brendan Jacobs for three years. Nice guy, but not overly bright—not like his daughter. He started making decisions that were at first odd, then downright bad for business. He didn't like being questioned about them, so I mentioned my concerns to his wife."

"What did she say?" Taney asked.

He almost heard MacKay shrug. "She didn't know a lot about the business, so she took her husband's word that everything was okay."

"But it wasn't," Taney suggested.

"He borrowed a lot of money to expand the plant, but ended up using it to fund cash flow. When the bank realized there was no asset securing the funds, they called in the loan."

Standard practice, Taney knew.

"Jacobs couldn't pay—the bank forced a sale of the business. I was the only person willing to buy it, and I wasn't willing to pay very much. Once the bank took what it was owed, there was nothing left over for the Jacobses."

Taney drummed his fingers on the desk. "Sandra doesn't see it that way."

"I wouldn't expect her to," Lundgren said briskly. "She doubtless thinks I should have tried harder to convince her mother there was a problem, but it wasn't my responsibility."

"Why did her father make such bad decisions?" Something didn't add up here.

"Turned out the guy had Alzheimer's," MacKay said.

"They didn't figure that out until a year later, but I'd say it caused his behavior."

Sandra's dad has Alzheimer's? Damn, he should have asked her about her parents' health at that dinner. It was obviously a sensitive subject—no wonder she'd gotten mad. The only comfort was that Taney's brother hadn't managed to ask that, either.

Alzheimer's disease would explain what had happened to the Jacobses' business. Lundgren had jumped on the opportunity her father's illness had presented, when instead, he could have tried harder to alert Sandra's mom, or even Sandra, to the situation. Lundgren's conduct was sleazy; Taney wouldn't have stooped to it. But it was legal.

"I'd like to meet to talk about the Will Branch sponsorship," Lundgren said. "How does tomorrow look?"

Sandra would never want to work for Lundgren, of course, even if Lundgren was happy to keep the existing publicity arrangements. She would be furious to know Taney was even talking to the guy.

He wouldn't tell her. Chances were, it would come to nothing, like all the other discussions they'd had with potential sponsors. And after what she'd done with Alyssa, he didn't owe her anything by way of open communication.

"Tomorrow's fine," he said. "How about ten o'clock?"

WILL'S ATTEMPT to qualify at Richmond ended in disaster. He started his qualifying lap at tremendous speed, taking advantage of the track's increased stickability thanks to the cool day. But his tires were cold, and he didn't give them enough work before he started his lap. In turns one and two, he held his line, but going fast into turn three, he spun out and hit the wall.

The car was wrecked, which meant the team would have to run with its backup car again for an unprecedented second time in just a few weeks, and Will would be starting at the back of the field—assuming NASCAR took pity on him and gave him a provisional entry to Saturday's race.

As Sandra watched the car being towed off the track, she hoped no one who had any interest in sponsoring Will was watching.

If there was anyone, anywhere who wanted to sponsor Will. Apart from Alyssa.

She glanced at Taney, standing distant from her where last week they'd cheered Will side by side. They'd barely spoken to each other since Talladega. She hadn't wanted to attend his meeting with Alyssa, and since they had no other active prospects, there was no need for her and Taney to meet.

It was painful to be on hostile terms with the man who held her future in his hands. Increasingly, alarmingly, it felt like more than her financial future.

She cursed her own susceptibility. The world was full of ordinary, gentle, family-minded men. Some of them were taller than Sandra. So why did she have to want Gideon Taney above all others?

Last week, she'd taken the opportunity to visit other clients, making sure her staff were delivering the service their customers expected. It was important, necessary…and yet being apart from Taney, knowing he was angry with her and that she deserved it, made every hour drag.

She was headed for the hauler when a voice behind her—like Taney's, but not—said, "Bad luck."

Steve Taney was at the track today, too. Sandra had exchanged a few words with him earlier, before he'd gone to watch qualifying with Taney. Steve was visiting Richmond on business and would fly home tonight, rather than staying on for the NASCAR Sprint Cup Series race. "It's no fun going to the race without Lisa," he'd told Sandra. Now, he eyed the battered No. 467 car. "How much do you think it'll cost to fix that?"

"I don't know, but you can bet it's scary."

Steve looked incongruous in the well-cut suit and silk tie he'd worn to his meetings. He was handsome and well-groomed, but he couldn't hold a candle to Taney, who was huddled with Will and Seth. Taney exuded authority even in his team polo shirt and faded blue jeans.

She turned her back on him and asked Steve, "How is Danielle?"

He groaned. "If you never see me or Lisa again it'll be because she's driven us into an early grave."

"That good, huh?"

"She's a hot-tempered, narrow-minded know-it-all."

Sandra was taken aback, and Steve grinned. "I can say that because she's my kid. You say it, and there'll be trouble."

Sandra laughed.

"Is that my favorite niece you're talking about?" Taney's stealthy approach from behind startled Sandra. She jumped, and Taney's hands instinctively came down on her shoulders to steady her. Then, obviously, he remembered he was mad at her, and he whipped his hands away.

"You can have Dani if you like her so much," Steve said with feeling.

"Just put her in a race car," Taney said. "I can't believe you're holding out on this."

Steve jerked back. "I wouldn't let my wife get in a race car, why would I let my daughter?"

"Because Dani is desperate to race, whereas Lisa would never do anything that might give her helmet-hair," Taney said.

Steve laughed reluctantly. "I know racing's about as safe as it can be when you get to this level—" he waved in the direction of the garage "—but no one makes it this far without their share of crashes."

"It's probably no riskier than horse riding," Taney said. Steve paled at the thought his precious daughter might ride a horse; Taney rolled his eyes. "She's a girl, not a china doll. Sooner or later, you have to let her take a risk."

Steve glared. "Thanks for your expert advice, Taney, but you don't know the first thing about kids, not even my kids. Especially not my kids, given you missed both their birthdays last year."

Taney's chin came out, and Sandra knew an argument was imminent. He didn't need this right now, not with the stress in the garage.

She put a hand on his arm; his head snapped around and he glared at her.

"Steve," she said, "Taney might not have much experience with kids, but he's a great judge of ability." His arm twitched beneath her hand. "Just look at those guys." She pointed to the Taney Motorsports team, working to prepare the backup car. Everyone was working fast, but not carelessly and without encroaching on each other's space. It was like watching a modern ballet as, before their eyes, the generic backup car was transformed into a machine that could win *this* NASCAR Sprint Cup Series race at *this* track.

"I'm looking," Steve said reluctantly, too polite to brush her off the way he had Taney.

"When Will wrecked his car during practice at Phoenix, the team fell apart. If Taney hadn't been there, I don't think the backup car would have been ready, let alone able to finish a race." She inched closer to Taney, despite his hostile vibes. "Every guy on that crew has had to fight for his place and only keeps it by being the best at what he does."

Steve nodded, clearly not as interested in where this was going as Taney, whose eyes were fixed on Sandra's face, querying, alert.

"Not only do the guys know they're the best, they all think they *know* best," she said. "When you have a panic on, it can get messy. At Phoenix, Taney judged everyone's abilities, and, more importantly, their attitudes. He knew who was making sound decisions, who could take the lead and who was going to have to swallow their pride and be a follower. Not only that, he managed to convince them all he was right. And you know what a turnaround we had out on the track."

"Huh." Steve looked at his brother with grudging respect. "I didn't know you still did that kind of thing."

Taney cleared his throat. "I've got back into it lately."

Sandra wasn't done yet. "Any NASCAR fan knows being a race car driver is about attitude as much as it is about ability. If Taney thinks Danielle can make it in a quarter midget, then you can bet he's taken everything into account—and that includes both her ability to be a great driver and the attitude that'll keep her safe."

Now she did look up at Taney, and the curious intensity in his eyes held her for several long seconds.

Steve snapped his fingers right in front of her face. "Break it up, you two. I'm still here."

Taney shook his head. "Sorry, Steve, I guess I got distracted." He grinned at Sandra, friendlier than he'd been since Talladega.

"Yeah, well, that reminds me, I've got the sexiest woman in the world waiting for me back in Boston—" Taney looked as if he might disagree with that, so his brother glared at him "—which means I'd better get to the airport."

He shook Taney's hand, kissed Sandra on the cheek, giving her shoulders a little squeeze as he did so.

"Thanks, guys, I'll tell Lisa your thoughts about Danielle." Then, interestedly, he asked, "Which do you think is cheaper, renting a car for the day to get here from the airport, or taking a cab?"

Taney groaned. "I have no idea. But I'm sure the cab driver will have strong views."

"You're right, cabbies have a lot of interesting things to say about money." Steve looked enlivened at the prospect.

After he'd left, Sandra said, "Taney, can I talk to you? It's important."

He didn't fob her off, even though they were so busy. "Let's go into the hauler."

Kylie Palmer was in the office area, writing up a statement for the press about Will's crash in qualifying. At Sandra's request, she left to continue her work in the media center.

Sandra sat, and, unlike the last time they'd met in the hauler—she realized with a shock it was only last week— Taney sat close to her on the banquette. His knee brushed hers under the table, then rested against it, strong and solid.

"Thanks for taking my side with Steve," he said.

"I told him the truth." She swallowed. "Which is something I haven't always done recently."

He twisted to face her, eyebrows raised.

"I'm sorry," she said. "I should have told you about Alyssa, no matter that I think she'd be a terrible sponsor. You were right, I wasn't practicing what I preach to you about openness and honesty." Ruefully, she added, "You must be so sick of my preaching."

He threaded his fingers through hers on the table and reestablishing physical contact with him was a balm to her soul. "Luckily, I like the sound of your voice."

She smiled. "Can you forgive me?"

He lifted her hand to his lips. "Of course. No one's right all the time, and you're right more often than I'm comfortable with anyway."

"Really?" She beamed.

"Why do I get the feeling I'm creating a monster?"

She said softly, bravely, "A monster who cares about you."

He slipped his arm around her shoulder, pulled her to him. Sandra felt a kiss against her hair. By Taney's side was the best place in the world. She said, "Will you come to a wedding with me?"

"Uh…" Taney's arm around her shoulders went rigid.

She giggled. "Danny Cruise's wedding is on Tuesday night—they had to schedule it when his fiancée's dad would be in town. Danny's a friend as well as a client, so I'm invited. Along with a date."

His arm relaxed. "I'd love to go." With a finger under her chin, he tilted her face. "I've missed you."

Sandra's cell phone rang, interrupting what was sure to have been a great kiss.

Ever the dedicated P.R. professional, she answered the call.

"What can I do for you, Bill?" Her voice was tight as she inched away from Taney. She listened for a moment, then said, "It was only twenty-four hours. I'm sorry, there have been a few difficulties, but everything is under control now."

"It won't happen again, Bill," Sandra said, feigning confidence.

Whatever the bank manager said next made her swallow and blink. "That's correct."

Then the conversation eased and she uttered a few platitudes about the Branch brothers' racing. When she ended the call, she stuffed the phone into her pocket and let out a shaky breath.

"Money trouble?" Taney's question startled her.

"I—what do you mean?"

"My start-up days at All Sports weren't that long ago. I can recognize a phone call from a bank manager. That's who is was, right?"

Her eyes widened, then she nodded jerkily. "I was a day late with my loan repayment. He's nervous."

"You're not the first small business owner to struggle with cash flow."

"No," she agreed. "When I approached the bank for a loan to buy out my business partner, I thought I was lucky to find a manager who's a rabid NASCAR fan. Bill had no trouble understanding the opportunity." She pushed her hair behind her ears. "Trouble is, when things go wrong, he knows enough to gauge the implications for Motor Media Group. And he knows Will and Bart have lost their sponsors."

Taney frowned. "Don't tell me your business depends on the Brat Pack?"

When he put it like that, Sandra thought, it sounded

hopeless. About to do her usual impression of a successful businesswoman oozing confidence, she realized it would be another deception.

Not that her financial situation was the business of any of her clients. But just possibly, it was Taney's business. If there was any hope for a relationship between them, she should tell him the truth.

She folded her hands on the tabletop. "I borrowed a lot of money to buy out Tom, my business partner. I knew cash would be a problem the first couple of years. I didn't know how big a problem—and I didn't know the fees for my parents' care would go up more than ten percent a year."

"Things are pretty tight," he suggested.

She didn't take the easy way out, technically truthful, which would be to agree with him.

"Taney, I'm desperate." Her voice wobbled. "If the twins don't find sponsors soon, I won't be able to make my loan repayment. I can make it next month—" she balked at telling him that payment would likely be funded by advances on her credit cards "—but after that…well, I don't want to think about it."

"I had no idea," he said slowly.

"The business is doing well," she assured him. "If I didn't have unusually high debt and crazy financial commitments, I'd be fine."

He stared down at her. "No wonder you're always after more money."

"I don't like constantly having my hand out, but it's the way I have to be."

"If your situation is so desperate, why did you turn Alyssa Ritchie away?" he asked. "Surely not just to sabotage my sale."

She rolled her eyes. "I told you, because it'll hurt Will."

"Are you saying you'd let your business go under just so you don't hurt Will Branch's feelings?"

"I'm saying I believe there's always a right way to do things. If you wait long enough, it'll come to you."

He looked troubled. "I hate the thought that when I sell the team—" she noticed he didn't say *if* he sold the team, so obviously his feelings hadn't changed sufficiently to solve one of her problems "—if the new owner doesn't want you to work for him, your company could go under."

"It's not your problem," she said. "It'll be my job to show him I can work with him—or her—and that Motor Media Group does great work to maximize sponsors' investments." Her fingers gripped the edge of the table. "If it's Alyssa, I'll have to figure out a way to respect her enough that I can work with her."

TANEY WOULD HAVE offered money to help Sandra out, if he'd thought she'd take it. But he knew she wouldn't. And looking at her, at the determination in her eyes as she spoke about working with Alyssa, no matter that she didn't want to, Taney believed she could do it. She was brave.

But she'd never be able to work with MacKay Lundgren.

CHAPTER FOURTEEN

WHEN SANDRA ARRIVED—late—at the team headquarters on Monday, Taney couldn't wait to give her some good news.

"We have Delacord Theaters coming in at eleven. They heard that Will Branch is bargain-basement stock, and they want a piece of the action."

"Perfect!" She high-fived him. "Just think how hunky Will would look blown up large on theater screens." Her grin said she was as happy as he was that they might have a prospect to displace Alyssa. Of course, she still didn't know about MacKay, who'd had a couple of meetings with Taney, and who showed every indication he was preparing a proposal.

"Delacord sounded as if they have more to spend than Alyssa," he told Sandra, and watched her eyes light up. Hopefully Delacord would outbid Lundgren, too.

Together, they brainstormed ideas on how to tailor their pitch to Delacord. Theater advertising, as Sandra said, was an obvious use of Will's sponsor time. But there were lots of other ideas, too—they were really sparking off each other today. Taney figured their productivity resulted from their mutual desperation to find a sponsor whose involvement wouldn't drive a wedge between them.

Will and the team hardly seemed the most important thing anymore.

Jay Nicholson from Delacord nodded and laughed and commented in all the right places during their pitch. He loved NASCAR, and he asked intelligent and aware questions. He thought Will Branch's "high-spirited" behavior would endear him to the company's younger demographic audience. And he had money—six million this year, more the next two—to spend.

He was a dream come true.

When he left—right after he said he was sure Delacord would submit a bid by the deadline next week—Taney hauled Sandra into a hug.

"You were great," he told her.

"You were better."

"*We* were fantastic."

They sealed their agreement with a kiss. It was as hot as ever—although they restrained themselves due to the possibility of someone walking in on them—but it had another dimension to it that Taney could only describe as *warmth*. Heat plus warmth didn't make much sense. But where heat could flare into either sexual passion or anger, warmth was constant and enduring.

He found himself envisioning how the future might pan out for him and Sandra, if they could get past their ups and downs. For the first time since Tess, he could imagine a relationship—*see, he didn't flinch at that word*—that might last for years. What the heck, why not admit where his thoughts were going? Maybe he and Sandra would get married one day. He could think of a dozen good reasons, right off the bat.

They'd have great sex—he couldn't wait to get started

on that—and they'd each have their businesses, which would sometimes allow them to work together. At home, they'd talk about all kinds of stuff, and he would value her opinions, even if he didn't always tell her so for fear of her getting a big head. She was so strong-minded, she'd try to push him around, but he was the one man who would never let her get the best of him. At least, not more than half the time.

"You know," he said against her hair, "if the world ended right now, I'd be a happy man." It was a way of telling her how important she was, without having to say something he wasn't ready for.

She tightened her arms around him, then she pulled away. "I'll bet you'd be happy," she said. "You'd get to re-populate the planet, and I'd get vaporized."

Taney blinked. "I'll get to *what?*"

SANDRA CLAPPED a hand to her mouth. *I can't believe I said that.* But Taney's comment had flustered her—did it mean what she hoped, that he'd be happy as long as he had her in his arms?

His eyes narrowed. "You said I'd get to repopulate the planet." He tightened his hands on her waist and said silkily, "What did you mean?"

"It's just a…stupid thought I had. Once."

"I'll judge if it's stupid." He leaned down and nipped her lower lip. "I'm the boss, remember."

He wasn't going to let her duck out of this.

"I just thought with you being so tall and strong and—" she met the keen intelligence in his eyes "—reasonably smart and…passably handsome—" He was laughing now and he looked downright devastating. "If some nuclear disaster ever wiped out the world, they might round up guys like you and put them somewhere safe."

"So that we can repopulate Earth."

"Uh-huh." She lifted her chin. "It's not such a stupid idea."

"Not at all," he said thoughtfully. "In fact, it has a certain genius." He rubbed his chin. "Do you think there's a list somewhere I can get my name put on?"

She slapped his arm. "No, I do not."

He caught her hand, pulled it to his lips, kissed her knuckles. "Did you ever think about what kind of women they—whoever *they* are—would provide to assist in this patriotic exercise?"

He nipped one knuckle, and sensation catapulted through Sandra. Breathless, she said, "I told you, I only thought about it once. Not for very long."

His chuckle said he didn't believe her. "I'm thinking they'd need tall, strong, smart, gorgeous, red-haired, stubborn—" he ducked the swipe she aimed at his shoulder "—women with childbearing hips. Ouch!"

Sandra had kicked his shin.

"You know I love your hips." His hands slid down to caress them through her skirt.

"You've never seen them," she said over the noise of her biological clock, which was suddenly ticking up a storm.

"I can fix that in an instant." He went for her zipper.

She twisted away, with a little shriek of outrage. "Not here, you can't."

"Then where?" he asked. "And when?" He tugged her against him. "Because, sweetheart—" his warm breath fanned the endearment over her "—I find I have a rather strong desire to…see your hips."

"If it's just to *see* them," she said nonchalantly, delighting in the sensual banter, "I could supply a photo."

"I like to employ all five senses in my seeing." His hands roamed her body. "Sight, touch…" His voice turned husky. "Taste…"

Sandra uttered a little mew of longing, then gave herself up to his kiss.

They both struggled to end it.

"When?" Taney asked again, his voice as shaky as she felt.

"It's Danny's wedding tomorrow night," she said.

"That's more than twenty-four hours away."

She laughed at the sweetness of his impatience. She hadn't thought it was possible to want Taney more than she had last week. But the past few days, since she'd apologized to him about Alyssa, their relationship had deepened, and with it had her desire. She knew he felt the same.

But although she'd opened up to him about her financial problems, the Sandra Jacobs he knew wasn't the real Sandra Jacobs. When he complimented her, it was always about how strong and smart she was. And beautiful, though that didn't matter. He didn't see a woman who desperately needed unconditional love that would last through thick and thin.

Before they made love, she needed to clue him in.

"Taney," she said, "am I like the other women you've dated?"

Taney recoiled. "What kind of trick question is that?" He shoved a hand through his hair. "I can't believe you're asking that at a time like this."

"It's just…most people have a pattern. A preference." She ran a finger along the hardness of his jaw. "I, as you know, veer toward the sensitive type." He snorted, and she snickered. "What sort of women do you veer toward?"

"I don't have any veering in mind right now, other than toward you," he said. "But I guess in the past, I've dated women who are independent. Successful. Strong. So, yeah, maybe there's a pattern. That doesn't mean I see you as being just like the other women I've dated."

He looked worried, and it touched her. "I didn't imagine that you do. Believe me, I don't think you're like any of the sensitive guys I've dated.

"The thing is, Taney," she said more seriously, "I'm not as strong and independent as you imagine. I'm more your needy kind of woman. I could even be…clingy."

TANEY ALMOST LAUGHED, but he could see Sandra had a bee in her bonnet. Which was no surprise, given the stress she'd been under at work. "I know you're worried about your business," he said. "But that's just money. I'd bail you out in a heartbeat, if you wanted me to." He would never begrudge her anything material. It wasn't as if she was asking for his *soul*.

"It's not just about money." She was chewing on her lip, and she looked adorable.

He loved that his strong, warrior woman could appear so fragile. But he was certain this was just a little insecurity on Sandra's part. Hard to understand, when she was such a phenomenal woman, but, hey, everyone had something they worried about. Sandra might fear that she wasn't strong enough for him, but Taney knew better. "You're incredible," he said, "and I want you."

On the table beside them, Taney's cell phone rang. He recognized the number of the Delacord Theater guy. "I'd better take this." He picked up the phone, dropped a last, quick kiss on her mouth. "We'll talk—et cetera—at the wedding tomorrow." He pressed the answer button. "Jay, what can I do for you?"

Sandra nodded, but she still looked uneasy as she left. Through the internal window, as he talked to Jay, Taney watched the sway of those luscious hips as she walked down the stairs. He wanted her so much. Tomorrow, he would have her. And they would take it from there.

No way was Sandra needy or clingy, no matter what she thought.

Hell, her idea of clinging was probably letting a guy make her a cup of coffee two mornings in a row.

She was perfect for Taney!

MacKay had called Alyssa several times since she last saw him. The first time had been to see if she needed any further help with her proposal to Taney Motorsports. He'd answered several questions for her.

Then the conversation had turned personal, and Alyssa had been shocked to realize they'd talked nearly an hour, though about what, she couldn't say.

His second call had been less pleasant. He'd phoned to insist she cancel the dinner with his mother. The opportunity to rile him had been too good to resist, so Alyssa refused. She still had no intention of going along, but she was having too much fun to tell him that.

On Friday, he'd shown up at her condo to tell her he didn't want her going to his mom's house. He'd dialed the number on his cell phone, handed it to her and told her to cancel.

Alyssa had enjoyed a very friendly five-minute chat

with Bettina Lundgren, ending it with a reiteration of how much she was looking forward to dinner on Tuesday.

MacKay had been incandescent—so much so that Alyssa hadn't been able to resist kissing him and he, to his obvious chagrin, hadn't been able to resist kissing her back.

He'd left with the furious comment that he'd doubtless be forced to see her at the Richmond NASCAR Sprint Cup Series race on Saturday.

He wished. Alyssa hadn't told him that Larry Preston had invited her to his suite for the day. She'd decided to let MacKay spend a frustrating day looking out for her, anticipating their next kiss.

Now, it was Tuesday morning, the day of Bettina's dinner. Alyssa couldn't wait to torture MacKay with the prospect she might actually turn up.

Six months ago, Danny Cruise would have been voted Driver Least Likely to Fall in Love. Then the ultimate loner had fallen head over heels for a woman he'd met in the off-season, and it seemed he couldn't wait to tie the knot.

Cruise was racing brilliantly this year—there was an edge to his driving Sandra hadn't seen before. It made her job as his publicity rep much easier. Danny put his dominant form down to happiness, and whenever Sandra saw him with Madison, his fiancée, she had to agree he was a changed man.

Danny was the hardest-working driver she knew, and that had meant a lonely life for him. He'd earned his happiness and Sandra was ready to celebrate at his wedding.

The ceremony was scheduled for four-thirty at the

historic Poplar Tent Presbyterian Church in Concord. The reception would take place at the track nearby.

Sandra had bought a new dress—midnight-blue silk, Grecian in style. The scooped bodice draped softly over her bosom, and the skirt fell from a high waist down to her knees.

"You look incredible," Taney said when she opened her door to him. He rested his hands on her hips, kissed her mouth. He looked good enough to eat, in his suit, and Sandra responded with enthusiasm. His mouth moved around to her ear, where he nibbled until desire arced through her and her hips jolted forward in an age-old message of longing. "I love that you're so tall," he murmured against her earlobe.

Her laugh was shaky. "Then I'd better not tell you one of my favorite fantasies."

That intrigued him enough to make him draw back. "Hmm." He kissed her again. "Right now, I can't imagine anything better than reality. But, out of academic interest, maybe you'd better tell me this fantasy."

"It's mine," she said, "it's nothing to do with you."

"I might be able to make it come true."

She laughed. "Not a chance."

He frowned. "You'd definitely better tell me. And that's an order. Tell me, Sandra."

"It's just that sometimes—" saying it out loud, it sounded so stupid that she ended up addressing the knot in his tie "—I like to imagine I'm…shorter."

"Interesting." He sounded thoughtful, but when she looked up, his eyes shone with laughter. "You mean, say, five-eight?"

"Shorter than that," she admitted.

"Five-five?"

"Shorter."

Silence. She looked up, to find incredulity written on his face.

He sighed. "How short?"

She hung her head. "I sometimes think it'd be fun to be five feet tall." At his snort, she added, "Maybe five-one or two. Five-three in my shoes."

He tsked. "That would make our job of repopulating the planet a lot more awkward." She shivered at the prospect of the joining with him. He tilted her chin up, then ran his gaze over her, top to toe. "Nope, for the sake of the planet you're better off how you are."

He kissed her again, parting her lips with his tongue. "See," he murmured against her mouth, "the height you are now makes this so easy."

"Height has nothing to do with it," she said. "*I'm* easy, where you're concerned."

He picked up the pashmina she'd left on the chair by the front door, and draped it over her shoulders. "I'm counting on it, sweetheart."

CHAPTER FIFTEEN

THE WEDDING SERVICE was as beautiful and as moving as every wedding should be. The bride, Madison, looked gorgeous in off-the-shoulder cream silk, and the love that blazed on Danny's face as she walked down the aisle gave Sandra a stab of envy so sharp she was ashamed.

When Madison reached the front of the church, Danny surprised everyone except his bride by hunkering down and giving a low whistle. At a pattering sound, the guests turned around in their pews, jostling to see the source of the noise. A puppy of indeterminate breed scampered down the aisle, a little basket around its neck. In the basket nestled a tiny cushion bearing two gold rings. Both Madison and Danny made a fuss of the dog, petting it as Danny retrieved the rings from their unusual bearer.

"Madison's a vet," Sandra whispered to Taney, who appeared taken aback by the canine member of the wedding party. "She and Danny met after Danny ran over a dog—a different dog, which is now back with its owner."

Taney nodded, clearly unconvinced that the couple's history necessitated the presence of a dog at their nuptials.

Sandra thought it was a nice touch. Because that accident with the dog had been the start of Danny's transformation from a man who thought about nothing but racing into a guy who could care for a pet. From there he'd become a man who couldn't wait to marry the woman he loved, and now, going by the look he had in his eyes these days when kids hounded him for autographs, he wanted to start a family.

Sandra shook her head. Could love really transform a man that much? She couldn't imagine Taney softening the way Danny had.

MACKAY'S MOTHER was a full foot shorter than he was— MacKay's height was reportedly inherited from his father—but she wrapped her arms around him in a strong squeeze that suggested she was no stranger to physical work.

The hug done with, Bettina looked past him. "Where's Alyssa?"

"She's not coming." *I hope.* The witch had phoned him six times today. First to say she was coming, then to say she wasn't, then she'd suddenly thought of a reason why she should come after all, then she had a headache and wasn't well enough. He hoped it was a three-day migraine.

MacKay had no idea if she would show up, but on balance, he was counting on the boredom factor—he loved having dinner with his mom but it would be unbearably tame to Alyssa—outweighing her desire to tick him off.

Dissatisfied, he glanced around the living room while his mother poured him a whisky. This was the biggest, most expensive house she'd allowed him to buy her, but he didn't think it was good enough.

Not after what Mom had been through raising MacKay and his five younger siblings. She deserved a palace. She was worth ten of Alyssa. Twenty.

But it was Alyssa who'd occupied his thoughts to the point of obsession the past couple of weeks.

"She sounds like an interesting young woman." Bettina handed him his drink.

"She's not young," he said sourly. "She just pretends to be." She got away with it, too.

His mom smacked his hand, the one that wasn't holding the drink. "Did I raise you to think it's okay to be rude about a lady?"

"She's not a—" He met his mom's glare and instead commented, "I don't think you'd like her."

"She sounds strong-minded," Bettina said. "I like that."

Too damned strong-minded. Alyssa had made him so mad the past few days—only the certainty that he would win the battle she had no idea he was waging against her kept him from throttling her. That and the fact that talking to her, sparring with her, kissing her, had somehow become the highlight of his day.

All part of the adrenaline rush, part of the game.

"Is that her?"

MacKay joined his mom at the window and cursed when he saw Alyssa getting out of her red BMW. She wore a long, dark coat, and his first thought was to wonder what she wore underneath it. If it was that white dress, that wouldn't be too bad.

"She's stunning," Bettina said approvingly.

"It's all fake." Damn, he didn't want her here. His mom knew he wasn't lily-white, but he took care not to expose her to the less savory aspects of his life. He wanted her to be proud of him, wanted to repay her hard work with the knowledge she'd done a good job.

Alyssa greeted his mother as if they were old friends, obviously to annoy Lundgren. Then she took off her coat.

Desire hardened inside him, matched measure for measure by fury.

Her dress was a meager scrap of stretchy silver fabric that barely covered her from chest to thigh. Strapless, it wrapped tightly around her, starting low enough to bare a generous amount of cleavage. It made her waist look tiny, her hips delectably curvy and her long legs sexy as hell in four-inch stilettos.

"Good grief," Bettina said. "I see what you mean about the 36D cup."

Alyssa smoothed her hands over her hips, forcing MacKay to watch their progress. "I hope I'm not over-dressed, but I bought this today and couldn't wait to wear it." She darted him a provocative look.

If she wore any less she'd be *un*dressed.

"You know how it is with clothes," she confided to Bettina.

"Not really," Bettina admitted.

MacKay eyed his mom fondly. Her stocky figure would never lend itself to Alyssa-style clothing, even if she had the money and the bad taste to buy them. His mother wore sensible smocks, T-shirts and pants. All of which covered her decently.

He knew Alyssa had chosen this getup to annoy him. So he couldn't let her believe she'd won.

"That dress would be more suited to Danny Cruise's wedding," he said. "But I guess you weren't invited."

Half the town was at tonight's wedding, including just about everyone involved in NASCAR. But mistresses weren't usually welcome at events that celebrated monogamy.

"Seems I'm just as much an outsider as you are," she said coolly.

MacKay didn't even know Cruise, so her dig didn't affect him. But it made him wonder if that's why she was here tonight—because otherwise she'd be at home on her lonesome.

After a round of drinks, they sat down to dinner—a simple roast chicken—in the dining room.

Bettina asked Alyssa about herself. "Do you have any children? Ever been married?"

Alyssa shuddered. "No."

"Why not? A beautiful girl like you would have no trouble finding a husband."

"It's not my scene."

"Did anyone ever ask you?" MacKay said.

Going by her hiss, he'd hit a nerve.

Bettina glared at him and patted Alyssa's hand across the table, which had MacKay's hackles rising. If Alyssa wasn't the kind of woman men married, that was her fault.

"Alyssa's always had a man to look after her," he said. "She's been Hilton Branch's *special friend* for some years." For his mom's sake, he toned down the language he'd have preferred to use.

"The man who stole all that money?" Bettina asked.

"Allegedly," Alyssa said sweetly. "For all his faults, Hilton was a generous *special friend.*"

To Alyssa, Lundgren said, "After my dad died, Mom scrubbed floors, every day, for years, to support us kids."

"I preferred the easy option," she said.

Bettina flicked MacKay with her napkin. "If I hadn't been as plain as a penny, I might have chosen another way."

"You would not," he said, shocked.

"There's no glory in callused knees," his mother said.

"There's glory in setting a good example for your kids." His siblings weren't as wealthy as he was. MacKay's work ethic matched his mother's, and he'd started working odd jobs when he was ten. But they all had good jobs, and they were all close to their mother.

"I was blessed with the best." As always, Bettina refused to take the credit. She patted Alyssa's cheek this time, as if the more she liked her, the more she doled out the same treatment to Alyssa that she gave MacKay. "A strong woman will always find a way to survive, dear."

Alyssa looked doubtful. "I'd do just about anything to avoid scrubbing floors for a living."

"You had it tough as a kid," Bettina guessed.

"It was just me and my mom, I never knew my dad." Alyssa forked a small mouthful of chicken. "We didn't have any money—mostly we lived in a trailer. Mom threw me out when I was eighteen—she caught me in bed with one of her boyfriends, so she had grounds. But he said he loved me, wanted to marry me. I thought I loved him back. Mom said I was a man-stealing tramp and tossed me out."

MacKay was shocked by the surge of rage at the thought of an older man seducing a fatherless eighteen-year-old. He could see the same anger on his mom's face.

"Did you ever make things up with her?" Bettina asked.

Alyssa shook her head. "She's in care now, she had a bad stroke a couple of years ago, and since then she's had several tiny strokes that worsen her condition a little each time. She's still lucid, according to the staff at the center, but I haven't visited."

"Who pays for her care?" MacKay asked.

"Not me." She sent him a mocking glance as she took

a sip of her wine. "Hilton does. Automatic payments from a bank account the investigators haven't found yet."

"If your mom's deteriorating you might want to make your peace with her," Bettina said.

Alyssa concentrated on separating a piece of chicken from its bone. "I'm not sure I want to."

"You probably don't," Bettina agreed. "But you will one day, and then it'll be too late. Do it while you can and you'll have no regrets. Fewer regrets," she amended.

Alyssa looked unconvinced.

"I'm not saying the split was your fault, quite the opposite," Bettina said. "I don't hold with what your mother did—if a woman can't take her child's side, who will? Now, my Mac here has had his ups and downs and I'll not say he's always been a model of good behavior, but he's always had my full support."

"Thanks, Mom," MacKay said, and meant it.

"If only you were any good at choosing women." His mom lightened the mood—she had the knack of knowing when she'd said enough and moving gracefully on.

MacKay had never had that kind of tact. But he went with her lead and protested, "I thought you were on my side."

"Just stating a fact, my darling." She turned to Alyssa. "I don't know why he keeps making the same mistakes, one wife after another, and not one of them strong enough to manage him."

"I don't need managing," he protested.

"It'll probably take someone either very stupid or exceptionally clever," Alyssa said.

His mom laughed. For no reason MacKay could see,

other than that they were both strong women, Bettina liked Alyssa a lot.

When the evening ended and Alyssa took her leave, Bettina said, "You must come again."

Over my dead body. MacKay told his mom he'd see Alyssa to her car. He shut the door behind him so she wouldn't hear.

"Stay away from my mother," he told Alyssa as he walked down the path behind her. If that dress was half an inch shorter... He blocked out the thought.

She hit the remote unlock for her car, then turned to face him. "You have no say over me. Maybe you'd better try and convince her I'm poison."

"She likes you," he said bitterly.

"It won't last," she assured him. "No man's mother has ever liked me."

"Mom's not like most mothers."

"No." She sounded...envious. Too bad, she didn't get to share MacKay's mom. Alyssa was as plastic as Bettina was real—some things just shouldn't go together.

"Kiss me good night," she said.

He growled, but he dragged her into his arms and kissed her hard. She responded instantly, setting him afire, and he pushed her up against the car, kissed her again, tasted her swollen lips.

He'd always thought her lips were too full, too lush, to be natural. "Is anything about you real?" he demanded. He threaded his fingers through the platinum-blond hair that was in no way natural, then ran his hands down over the curves barely covered by that ridiculous excuse for a dress. "Is any of this real?"

Something that might have been hurt flared in her eyes.

Then they hardened. "It's as real as your willingness to help me with this NASCAR deal," she said. "So, you tell me."

He released Alyssa so suddenly that she would have sagged if she hadn't remembered her backbone in time. The illusion tonight—sitting down to eat together as part of a family—was just that, an illusion. MacKay hoped she could see that.

He watched as she got in her car and drove away, without looking back.

Then he stormed back into the house, slammed the door behind him.

"Don't invite her here again," he ordered his mother, knowing nothing he said would make any difference. "I can't stand that woman."

Bettina sent him a sly look. "She strikes me as exceptionally intelligent."

It wasn't until later that he remembered where he'd heard that phrase before. He cursed. And tried to put Alyssa out of his mind. And failed. Again.

THE WEDDING GUESTS at the reception held at the Charlotte racetrack were mostly NASCAR people. Among others, Taney talked to Dixon Rogers, owner of Fulcrum Racing, driver Dean Grosso and his wife, Patsy, and Richard Latimer, who was ebullient about his chances of signing EZ-Plus Software "any day now" to sponsor Bart Branch.

Taney must tell Sandra the good news.

He looked for her across the room, and when his eyes found her his heart beat faster.

Weddings were dangerous places for a guy to start thinking mushy thoughts about a woman—there was always something in the air, like a virus, that seemed to lead to a rash of engagement announcements in the weeks following the occasion.

Strangely, that thought didn't scare Taney. In fact, he quite liked it. Did thinking about marriage mean he loved Sandra? Taney tasted the thought, and found it wasn't too unpalatable. Huh, maybe he did love her. Not that sappy, can't-live-or-breathe-without-you love—he'd never seen the point of that—but something real, something two strong, independent people could work with.

He realized he couldn't go another minute without holding her in his arms, so he asked her to dance. She was light, and yet real and substantial in his hold. They moved together in a rhythm that was nothing fancy, but it worked.

That was what love should be like, Taney thought.

During one slow number, they ended up dancing along-side Danny and Madison.

"Hey, Taney, may I cut in?" Danny said.

"You have your own woman now," Taney growled.

"Yeah, but I plan to be inaccessible to anyone but my wife and my team owner and crew chief the next couple of weeks—" that was the trouble with a midseason wedding, the happy couple didn't get to honeymoon "—so I'd like to cover off a couple of things now with my P.R. rep." Danny dropped a kiss on Madison's mouth. "Excuse me, darling, I'll be right back." He took such a long time letting her go that Sandra laughed.

DANNY AND SANDRA danced, loosely clasped.

"You sure lucked out with Madison," Sandra told him.

"Yep." The driver whose rare smiles had, in the past,

always held a trace of bitterness or loneliness now lit up like a racetrack for a night race. "I never thought I could be both a race car driver and a good husband, but meeting Madison showed me I had no choice. She's everything to me."

"The relationships you had before..." Sandra felt tactless bringing up the subject of Danny's supermodel-dating history at his wedding, but she needed to know. "They were different?" Just how far could love change a man?

"About as different as a road course from an oval track," Danny said. "I was pretty selfish in those days, though I never saw it that way. But I'd do anything for Madison, and I never want to do anything without her."

It was about as far from *Every man for himself* as it was possible to get.

IT WAS NEARLY TWO in the morning when Taney drove Sandra back to her cottage.

By which time, every nerve in her body pulsed with anticipation—both desire and fear. She'd encouraged him to think they would make love tonight...but she still hadn't been as open with him as she should.

"That was a great night." He took her key from her, unlocked the door.

"Yeah." Sandra snapped on the lights on the way to the kitchen. "Danny and Madison are so happy. If I ever get married, I hope it's to a guy who looks at me the way Danny looks at Madison."

Taney snorted.

"What?"

"Marriage isn't about sappy looks."

She raised an eyebrow. "What is it about?"

"I'm not saying I'm an expert," he hedged.

"No, go on, I'd like to hear this." She put the kettle on the stove.

"We've talked enough," he said. "I need to kiss you. Right now." He pulled her into his arms, into a kiss that explored every nuance of her mouth.

Eventually, behind them, the kettle boiled.

Taney loosened his embrace. "How about that coffee?"

Sandra palmed her cheeks to cool them. "It seems to me you have no need of further stimulation."

"You're right. All I need is you." He kissed her again, and his hands moved down her body with increased urgency. He slipped one leg between hers, bringing them even closer together. "You're so beautiful," he said. "So delicate."

Delicate! Sandra almost laughed, yet the reverence with which he cupped her face so he could kiss her eyelids, her nose, then her lips—gently this time but just as demanding—did make her feel delicate.

He sighed against her mouth. "I'm crazy about you, Sandra. Please, sweetheart, let me show you. Let me make love to you."

He'd said, *I'm crazy about you.* Sandra's heart said in return, *I love you.*

It was true; the words sang in her head. She'd fallen in love with Gideon Taney. With that take-charge strength of his, with that vulnerability he didn't know he possessed and certainly wouldn't thank her for mentioning, with his uncompromising integrity…he'd captured her heart.

Sandra entwined her arms around his neck, planted a kiss on those firm lips. The heat rose faster than before.

Taney began to walk her backward, out of the kitchen. "Is your bedroom this way?"

"Yes, but—"

"Mmm, yes, butt," he joked, his hands molding her bottom. She loved this playfulness that he didn't show to anyone else but her. She wanted to play with him the rest of her life.

TANEY GROANED with the sensation of Sandra's curves crushed against his chest. This woman drove him nuts—he had to have all of her, to make her his, right now. The primitiveness of the urge shocked him.

"Taney…" Her hands slipped beneath his shirt. Her palms were cool against his back. "This isn't just sex, is it?"

"No, sweetheart, this is a lot more than sex." He found the right room and walked her into it.

She resisted his momentum, and he bumped into her. "Taney, you need to know, I'm looking for a man who'll…cherish me."

"*Cherish* you?" He chuckled against her hair at the incongruousness of his six-foot warrior woman saying she wanted to be cherished.

"I can't let this go further," she said, "without being completely honest."

She twisted out of his embrace with a suddenness that suggested she wasn't as caught up in the moment as he was. Taney stifled a groan.

"Taney, my father has Alzheimer's."

"I know, sweetheart."

She looked puzzled, and he remembered Lundgren was the one who'd told him. "I heard. I should have asked you about it, and I'm sorry."

Sandra sat down on the king-size bed, where, although he hadn't lost hope, it now seemed increasingly unlikely they were going to end up tonight. She knotted her fingers in her lap. "I'm afraid I'll end up like Dad."

Relief flooded Taney. "Sweetheart, Alzheimer's isn't hereditary." He sat down next to her, stroked her hair. "Sure, you might get it, but so might I. We can't worry about what's going to happen when we're seventy, or eighty."

"My dad is only sixty-seven," she said in a small voice. "He hasn't recognized me in years. His Alzheimer's is what they call early-onset. He was fifty when it was diagnosed—but it can start much younger."

Taney's hand stilled in her hair. "What are you saying?"

"Taney," she said, loud and clear now, "early-onset Alzheimer's is genetic, and the gene can be passed on from parent to child. From Dad to me." She took a deep breath. "If I sleep with you, it'll be because I think we have a future together. If you're thinking the same, then you need to know there may come a day when I don't recognize you. And it might not be that many years away."

Stunned, Taney let his hand drop. Sandra's longing to find a sensitive guy, her talk of being clingy, her inexplicable insecurity, had all been about this.

Hell, she was a walking time bomb!

Could Taney care for her, maybe for years, when she no longer knew him, no longer knew herself? Did the love he felt for her go that far? Automatically, his hand resumed stroking her beautiful hair. She snuggled against him, and suddenly he was conscious of the weight of her leaning on him, of the strength in her grip on his shoulders.

He had his answer.

The love Sandra wanted—needed—wasn't the strong, independent kind of love Taney had to offer.

The threat of Alzheimer's was only a part of it. When he thought—really thought—about the things she'd said about his past relationships…he knew she needed a deeper, more embracing love in all aspects of her life.

Taney had spent his whole life avoiding that kind of love. At first unintentionally, when his parents had been forced to leave him and Steve in the U.S.A. while they worked in trouble spots. He'd loved his parents and he knew they loved him, but he couldn't afford to depend on their love. And it was a good thing he hadn't, because they'd died before he was really a man.

When he'd married Tess, he'd made a subconscious choice that he wanted the same uninvolved love in his marriage. When Tess had died, a part of Taney had been glad that he hadn't loved her more. That while he'd grieved, he hadn't been torn apart.

He imagined the awful pain of seeing Sandra, still alive, but slipping away from him. It hurt so much, just in that fleeting instant, that he couldn't see how anyone could choose to have that pain in their life.

He shifted away from her, but took both her hands loosely in his. "It's not definite, is it?" he said. "You might never get Alzheimer's." Because he couldn't accept their relationship could be over before it had really started.

Her gaze slid away from his. "If I did," she said, "would you be there for me?"

For one crazy second he wanted to tell her, yes, he'd be there for her, yes, he wanted to take care of her, no matter what. "I don't know," he said honestly. He released her hands. "I guess I need to figure that out."

She didn't say anything, and for a long while, neither of them moved. Then he stood, and she did, too.

"Good night, Sandra."

When he left, he didn't kiss her. It was a long time since kissing her had felt casual. Now, that intimacy would feel like a statement he wasn't sure he wanted to make.

CHAPTER SIXTEEN

SANDRA ASKED Kylie Palmer to handle all Will's public-
ity activities at Darlington. She couldn't be around Taney.
Instead, she worked with Bart's rep, Anita Wolcott.
Richard Latimer introduced her to the chief executive of
EZ-Plus Software, who confirmed his company was lined
up to sign an agreement on Bart's sponsorship tomorrow.

Sandra should have been thrilled. But nothing mattered—not even her business—compared with the loss of
Taney.

She berated herself for her naiveté in clinging to the
hope that he would somehow, as he put it, "figure this out."
Taney didn't get involved at an intimate level. He'd told
her, he'd showed her—how much evidence did she need?
She'd been deluding herself for weeks, and she still was.

Instead of watching the race in the pits with him, she
adjourned to the media center with Kylie.

For once, the roar of the cars as they passed the green
flag failed to excite Sandra, even though Will had qualified an impressive fourth.

"Taney gave Will an amazing pep talk," Kylie said. "I've
never seen him so emotional about a race. It got my blood
pumping, and I'm guessing it's done the same to Will."

Even hearing Taney's name hurt. Sandra realized now

that she'd secretly taken a chunk of the credit for Taney's more inspired speeches at the track. Sometimes she'd felt as if Taney was giving them just for her.

Another delusion.

TANEY HAD THOUGHT he wouldn't be able to concentrate on the race, knowing Sandra was here somewhere, but not by his side. It just felt wrong.

But Will started the race with a couple of swift passes that had everyone paying more attention than usual to the No. 467 car, and Taney found himself engrossed in his driver's progress.

On lap thirty, Will earned the track's famous Darlington Stripe—he brushed the wall in the tight second turn, and his car came away with a stripe of the wall's paint. Taney's heart was in this throat—could Will keep control of the car? So often he'd spun out in this kind of situation.

But Will kept his head and his car was undamaged. The incident didn't seem to hold him up.

Taney needed to be closer to the action, so he put on a headset that would allow him to talk to Will.

Two-thirds of the way through, Will called through to Seth that the car was overheating. His frustration was palpable—and with Will, frustration often led to risky driving and a crash.

"Take it easy, Will," Taney said into his radio.

"Taney?" Will hadn't realized he was hooked up. "This is a, uh, darned pain."

Well done on avoiding the curse.

"Seth is right. You're going to have let a couple of guys get past you," Taney said. Will made a sound of protest.

"We'll fix you up better than new when you pit. But for now, get the car back here in one piece."

Taney kept Will talking, which prevented him from taking matters into his own hands with a hotheaded charge that would likely blow up the engine. Three laps later he was able to pit under a caution.

It was a longer than normal pit stop, but it solved the problem. Will hit the gas with a vengeance, but tempered by good sense. He took advantage of a couple of late cautions to regain the places he'd lost, and finished the race second behind Dean Grosso.

It was a wonderful result—and it filled Taney with a strange mix of elation and loneliness. Since he'd left Sandra's house the other night, his emotions had been so raw, so exposed, that every sense was heightened. It was both painful and somehow exciting. When he'd given Will his prerace pep talk, the excitement had dominated. And when Will had been stuck with that overheating problem, Taney had shared his pain.

The race had been cathartic.

Taney didn't know how it had happened, but he'd dropped a load of baggage during those few hours—it had slipped away without his noticing.

And now, he made a decision.

HIDING FROM TANEY was a short-term strategy. A quitter strategy. And unlike Gideon "Every Man For Himself" Taney, Sandra wasn't a quitter.

By Monday morning, the day after the Darlington race, she'd wallowed long enough. Today was the closing date for the offers on Will's sponsorship; they were expecting proposals from Alyssa Ritchie and Delacord Theaters.

Sandra prayed Delacord's offer would be higher than Alyssa's.

She arrived at team headquarters at eleven o'clock. Taney wasn't in the mezzanine meeting room. Lately he'd taken to spending an hour or so in the shop on Monday mornings. The team appreciated it.

When he walked into the room ten minutes later, he immediately shrank it with his presence.

"You're here." No awkwardness, no break in his stride, no hesitation in his smile—was he that unaffected by the rift between them?

"Our sponsorship auction closes today," she said uncertainly.

"So it does." He sounded as if he'd forgotten, as if he didn't care.

"Taney, what's going on?"

He grabbed her hands, and now she saw a light of excitement in his eyes. "Good news. Taney Motorsports is not for sale."

It took a moment for the words to sink in. "Since when? Why not?"

"Since yesterday, and because—" he squeezed her hands "—I've realized you were right. I'm not going to quit because I've lost the buzz, I'm going to get the buzz back. I'll do what it takes to make it happen."

"That's great." Her head swam with the unexpectedness.

He drew her into his arms. "The team is a start," he said. "But I know there needs to be more."

She pulled back to look at him. "You mean…us?"

He nodded. "I hurt you the other night, and I'm sorry. I know I need to change my relationships, how far I get involved. I'm going to work on that."

He looked at her expectantly.

"I'm not sure what you're saying," she offered.

He let go of her, and he sounded a little annoyed as he said, "I want to be the man you need, that's what I'm going to work on. I'm going to learn to engage."

It was a logical, Taney approach. It was hopeless.

"How you learn to engage," she said, "is by doing it. Jump in to a relationship, make it happen—just like you're doing with the team."

"This is a lot more important than the team," he said. "I don't want to hurt you."

"If you jump in and do it, you won't hurt me."

It was so simple, but he didn't see it, she knew by the shake of his head. He was so pigheaded!

Or else he just didn't love her enough.

"Taney, I don't think—" She broke off as the meeting room door opened. The Taney Motorsports receptionist walked in, holding up two delivery packs. "I brought these, I know you're waiting for them."

"Thanks, Sally," Taney said distractedly. He didn't move, so Sandra took them from the woman.

She scanned one of the packages. "This one's from Alyssa. So this other one must be Delacord's." She squinted at the small type on the label of the second package.

Taney galvanized into action. "I'll take that." He grabbed the second pack.

"It's not from Delacord," she said, puzzled.

"Delacord called on Friday—there's been a takeover bid for the company, so all major commitments have been put on hold."

"So, who are First Rate Auto Loans?" She'd just managed to read the name before he took it from her.

He tossed the package on the table and ran a hand around the back of his neck. "I should have told you, but I didn't think it would get this far. It's a division of Lundgren Group."

The hated name assailed her ears. "*MacKay* Lundgren?" Her voice caught. Taney couldn't...he wouldn't...

He nodded.

He already did.

"You...you've been talking to MacKay Lundgren?" Her voice quavered.

"He approached me, similar to the situation with you and Alyssa."

"Alyssa didn't wreck your parents' lives." With shaking hands, Sandra tore the cardboard tab to open the unopened package and pulled out Alyssa's proposal. She jumped straight to the numbers. Who would have believed a day would come when she would welcome Alyssa's sponsorship? "Five million dollars this year, six million next, an option to renegotiate after that," she said tersely. Not good. "What's Lundgren got?"

Taney stepped between her and the table. "I don't want to talk about Will Branch's sponsor, dammit. I want to talk about you and me, our future."

Couldn't he see what he'd done? She reached around him for the UPS package and opened it. "Six mil this year, seven million a year for the next two years." She gripped the pages tightly until her knuckles whitened. "Are you going to take it?"

"Look, Sandra..." he said, overly reasonable.

She knew exactly what that tone meant. *This is business. Every man for himself.*

"I talked to Lundgren about what he did to your family,"

Taney said. "He told me he tried to convince your mom something was wrong with your dad."

"He made *one* comment to her *one* time." She sounded shrill, but she didn't care.

"I don't agree with his conduct, but there are plenty of others who would have done the same."

"It's not about that," she said, almost whispering now. "I don't expect you to despise Lundgren just because I do. But I want your full support in everything, no matter how unreasonable that sounds."

"Sandra…" He spread his hands, as if he had no idea how to commit on that scale.

"I love you, Taney." She saw his face light up, and pushed on. "But I don't want you unless you're willing to jump in, all the way, right now. I'm not going to wait for you to figure out whether or not you have it in you to love me."

She ran her hands over her face, pushed her hair back. "I don't know what the future holds for either of us, but I need to know that whatever life throws at me, you'll be there. Just like I'll be there for you, for the rest of my life if you're willing to do it my way. It's all or nothing."

She saw the shock in his eyes, and she drew a deep breath. "That's why I'm quitting the Taney Motorsports account." She'd only decided just now, but she knew it was right.

"That's crazy," he barked. "You can't afford to quit. We can work this out."

"I can't afford to get my heart broken." She swiped at the corner of one eye. "You told me your wife loved you too much to ask everything of you. Well, I love you too much not to."

He recoiled, then he came back mad, his chin jutting forward. "You can't give up on us—I love you, dammit. I haven't said that to anyone in over fifteen years—it's a big damned deal."

It was no deal, and deep down, he must know that. It hurt so much, she wanted to go home, climb into bed, pull the duvet over her head and never come out again.

Her cell phone rang and it was a sign of how screwed up her thought processes were that she automatically answered it.

"Sandra, this is Dr. Zakursky's receptionist."

It was the last straw. She burst into tears. Taney made a shocked movement toward her, and she turned away. "Tell Dr. Zakursky I forgot," she sobbed into the phone. "I'm sorry, I'll have to—" Then a tiny corner of her brain that was still rational pointed out how insane it was to reschedule a doctor's appointment in the middle of this. She switched off the phone.

"Tell me what's going on with that doctor, Sandra." Taney was getting overbearing, probably to hide his guilt at not being able to love her the way she loved him.

She pulled a tissue from her purse, blew her nose hard. And again. She lifted her chin.

"Taney," she said, "I quit."

FROM THE WINDOW that faced out on to the parking lot, Taney watched Sandra walk to her car. She stumbled halfway, as if blinded by those shocking tears, but she got there in the end.

He told himself she was the one who'd blown it. He'd given her his best offer, more than he'd offered anyone, even Tess. It was a commitment that he would be a better person for her—and she'd turned it down.

Why couldn't she accept there was only so much a guy could do at once? That if he took it one step at a time, he could probably handle it, but right now, she was asking too much?

Yet as much as he told himself she was unreasonable, he couldn't erase the picture of her crying, fumbling with that damned cell phone, as she talked to that doctor for what seemed like the thousandth time.

He flung away from the window, not willing to watch her car drive out of the lot. Why was she seeing a doctor anyway, when she kept insisting she wasn't sick?

Was Sandra sick? Fear clenched around Taney's heart and he raced to the window to call her back. She was gone. But that didn't mean she could keep fobbing him off. What was the doctor's name? Something weird. Zamorsky…Zakovsky…He strode to his laptop and began searching the Internet for a list of Charlotte doctors. It didn't take long. There he was. Dr. Anton Zakursky. Specialist in dementia.

Dad was diagnosed when he was fifty, but it can start much earlier.

The full import of those words punched Taney.

Sandra wasn't worried that she might one day get Alzheimer's. *She already has it.*

Wouldn't she have told him, if that was the case? No, because he hadn't asked, dammit, and she had a history of drip-feeding him those details of her life that made her seem less than the strong, independent woman he'd believed her to be: that her business was in trouble, that her parents relied on her to pay for their care, that her father had Alzheimer's, that his condition was hereditary.

Taney sagged into his chair, tried to absorb what had to

be the truth. There was no relief that he'd learned it just in time, that he'd been spared a life of caring for a sick woman. There was only pain, scalding, burning pain that seared away the layers of caution, of detachment, of self-protection.

Not pain for what he had lost, but for what Sandra would lose. He'd told her he didn't know if he could be there for her if the worst happened. Now he'd learned the answer in the hardest possible way.

He thought of how his strong, warrior woman had wept, and knowing it was his fault, he wanted to weep, too.

No time for that. He could see the way forward, so clear it dazzled him. He had a long list of things to do before he could take Sandra in his arms again.

He picked up the phone, and completed the first item on the list. He called MacKay Lundgren...and made a deal.

CHAPTER SEVENTEEN

NOTHING STAYS A SECRET very long these days. Alyssa heard the news about MacKay's offer to sponsor Will Branch at nine o'clock Tuesday morning.

The biggest surprise was not that he'd betrayed her…but how much it hurt. Had she really been naive enough to think he felt something for her? Had she been stupid enough to let herself fall for him?

Yes and yes.

Alyssa poured herself another cup of coffee from the pot on her kitchen counter. With a finger, she hooked the front of her little black tank, and peeked inside. The way she'd been acting, anyone would think she kept her brain in her bra. Somewhere under the flesh that men like MacKay so coveted was her heart. Still intact, of course. What was the point of having a ten-thousand-dollar body if it didn't provide a buffer between your heart and the outside world?

Ruthlessly, she discarded the tender thoughts about MacKay that had somehow trespassed across her cynicism—she should have thrown them out long ago. All was not lost, she told herself. She was one step ahead of MacKay. She still had Plan B.

As SANDRA EXITED the elevator on the first floor of the advanced care facility at Sunny Hills on Wednesday, the elevator opposite opened, too. A stunning blonde stepped out, wearing a hot pink, low-cut bustier-style dress that would likely give most of Sunny Hills' male residents an instant heart attack.

"Alyssa?"

Alyssa's glance flicked over Sandra. "Hello," she said without enthusiasm.

"Were you looking for me?" Sandra realized right away it was a stupid question, but maybe her office had told Alyssa she was here, and the woman wanted to complain about being cut out of Will's sponsorship.

"This isn't the first place I'd look for you," Alyssa said. "You're a little haggard, but I wouldn't have said you're a candidate for Sunny Hills yet." She glanced around the perfectly pleasant reception area and shuddered. "My mother's a patient here."

"So is my dad."

Alyssa said with a sneer, "Who would have thought we'd have so much in common? But I expect you're the devoted kind of daughter who's here all the time. Whereas I haven't been in a while."

"How was your mom today?"

Alyssa's mouth tightened. "She called me a slut and said she wished I'd never been born."

Sandra gasped, put a hand to her mouth. "I'm so sorry. Alzheimer's patients can get very abusive—the fact that it's part of the disease doesn't stop it hurting."

Alyssa smiled faintly. "Mom doesn't have Alzheimer's. She's been calling me a slut since I was eighteen years old. I wasn't really expecting to hear anything else, but I had some things I thought I'd better get said." She looked annoyed with herself, as if she wished she hadn't admitted that much.

"Oh." Sandra bit her lip.

"Our moms, what they think of us—if you don't mind me bracketing myself with you for one moment…" Alyssa smirked, but it seemed halfhearted. "Our moms' opinions have a lot of power over us. Today I took that power back."

"Good for you…I guess."

Alyssa read the worry in Sandra's tone. "Don't bother feeling sorry for me. My next wave of sordid revelations about Will's father will be out next week and you'll hate me all over again." She turned the smile into a full-on dazzler, tossed her gorgeous blond hair and, with a wiggle of her hips, stalked out of the building.

Sandra headed to her mom's apartment. She stopped outside the door while she tried to banish the gloom that must show on her face. For one awful moment, her father's oblivious forgetfulness seemed almost something to envy.

Ashamed of herself, she pushed open the door and called out a cheery greeting.

"In here, dear," her mother called from the living room.

Patricia Jacobs sat in one of two blue velvet-upholstered wing chairs that flanked an oak veneer coffee table. Her hands rested lightly on the chair's arms and her head was pressed back into the padding as if she was about to take off. Sandra recognized her mom's tired look.

"Bad night?" she asked. Her mom's health was generally okay for a woman of sixty-eight, but she was asthmatic, and when she suffered an attack in the night it left her exhausted the next day.

Patricia smiled and nodded. It took her a moment to summon the energy to say, "Much better now, just taking it easy."

"I'll make us some tea." Sandra headed to the small kitchen area, set the kettle to boil.

She'd brought her mom's favorite pastry, an apricot Danish. Patricia would insist they share it, so Sandra cut off a quarter for herself. Not out of selflessness, but purely because she couldn't afford to have that many calories land on her hips.

Taney would say he loved her hips, and would feed her another Krispy Kreme.

Damn him.

She carried the tea to the living room, glad for her mother's grateful smile, and sat down on the couch that had been part of the family as long as she could remember. It had been re-covered at least twice, and was now dark brown corduroy.

"The attack last night wasn't too severe," Patricia said. "But I couldn't get back to sleep. I was fretting."

There was only one thing Sandra's mother fretted about.

"When I think how ill your father is—" her mom's hands clenched on the arm of the chair "—I just know he wouldn't be so bad if MacKay Lundgren hadn't robbed us."

The last person Sandra wanted to think about. After Taney.

Sandra didn't know if the progress of Alzheimer's disease could be hastened by stress. But her mom was convinced of it.

"Don't think about MacKay, Mom. You give him too

much power over your life, your happiness. We both do. It's time to claim it back."

Her mother stared. "You've never said that before."

"I heard it from—" Sandra winced "—an up-and-coming lifestyle guru."

"You may be right," Patricia said thoughtfully. Then, unable to resist one final dig, she added, "But I still say Lundgren should have told me how serious your father's mistakes were."

"He should," Sandra agreed. But lots of people didn't do what they *should*.

TANEY FOUND HIS BROTHER at work in his CPA practice in downtown Boston.

He stood in the doorway of Steve's office and for a brief moment it was like looking in a mirror. He saw the years on Steve, the deepening grooves that ran from his nose to his mouth, the hairline a little higher than it had been. Taney hadn't noticed age encroaching, but he figured it must be doing the same to him.

"Hey, Kid." It was a long while since he'd used the nickname that had bugged the heck out of his brother when they were young. The one-year age gap between them had, according to Steve, been designed to ensure Taney got to do all the good stuff first. Taney thought about his brother's wife and family, and figured Steve must know by now that wasn't true.

Steve's head jerked up. For a bare moment, Taney saw surprised pleasure in his eyes, then it switched to the guarded affability he'd grown accustomed to. "I wasn't expecting you, was I? Or am I getting forgetful in my old age?"

Memory loss wasn't exactly Taney's favorite subject right now, but he smiled anyway. "Just a flying visit."

Steve walked around the desk to shake Taney's hand. Taney hauled his brother into a hug. Steve resisted, which wasn't how Taney had envisaged this moment, but then his brother awkwardly returned the embrace.

"How're Lisa and kids?" Taney asked.

"Okay. I mean, great." Steve shook his head as if to clear away confusion. "Why are you here?"

Taney shoved his hands in his pockets. "I came to see you."

"You didn't call."

"Do I have to?"

"No, but you always give us notice of a state visit." It was a joke, but it fell flat. "Sorry," Steve said. "I didn't mean—"

"You did mean it, and you're right," Taney said. "I've been acting like a jerk, forgetting that you guys are the most important people in my life." He grinned. "Well, you used to be, until recently."

A slow smile spread across Steve's face, and he looked more like the kid brother who'd plotted what had at the time seemed hilariously original mischief with Taney. Things like putting salt in their parents' coffee on April Fools' Day. That was before the boarding-school years, when they'd been, Taney realized now, a pretty close-knit family. At any rate, his mother and father had bravely taken great gulps of the coffee they were both smart enough to know had been rigged. Their sons making a cup of coffee for the first time ever, and it just happened to be April Fools' Day?

"We need to talk," Steve said. "Let's go out."

At a café around the corner, they sat at a table by the

window, with the spring sunshine filtering through wooden louvers.

"Do you know why I got interested in NASCAR?" Taney stirred sugar into his espresso.

"Because it's the best damned racing in the world." Steve sounded as if he was stating the obvious.

"Nope. Well, yeah, it is, but the first time I watched it with you on TV, I couldn't see the attraction."

Steve looked at him as if Taney had just declared the First Amendment to be a communist manifesto.

"I was wrong, obviously," Taney said. "But I didn't realize that for a couple of months."

"But we watched it together every week," Steve said. "Lisa and I were living in that apartment in Charlotte, and the three of us used to crowd onto that ratty couch—"

"You loved the excuse to squish close and keep your hands all over Lisa," Taney said, remembering.

"Yeah." Steve waggled his eyebrows. "Sometimes I wish we didn't have two couches these days. But are you telling me you didn't enjoy those Sunday afternoons?"

"They were the best thing in my life," Taney said simply. He leaned forward, clasped his hands on the table. "Steve, you and I had gone different ways before that. After Tess died, I got interested in NASCAR because it seemed the only way to get to know you again."

Steve looked intrigued. "Really?"

"By the time I started the team, I was nuts about the sport. But at the beginning, it was a way to spend time with you, and it worked. I'd never felt so close to you before."

"Or since," Steve suggested.

Taney nodded. "I lost that closeness. Or, rather, I gave it away." He spread his fingers on the table's polished wood surface. "I'd made the effort to get to know you and Lisa, and I assumed that was all I had to do to keep the relationship going. Then I got to love NASCAR, so I set up the team…and somewhere along the way you and I grew apart again."

Steve nodded. His eyes, greener than Taney's, were alight with curiosity.

"I ducked out of the relationship," Taney admitted. "Someone told me recently that I don't know how to engage fully with the people I love."

"That someone wouldn't happen to be the lovely Sandra?"

Taney grinned at his brother. "She's right, I don't. But I plan to change that, and I want to start with you."

Steve looked faintly worried. "We don't have to hug every time we see each other, do we?"

Taney laughed. "Maybe every couple of months. Can you live with that?"

Steve shrugged. "I'll have Lisa stand in for me sometimes."

"Great idea," Taney said with a pretend enthusiasm that had his brother punching him on the shoulder. "Steve, you've tried to talk to me plenty of times, and I haven't wanted to hear it. From now on, I'm going to listen. Hell, I'm going to answer my damned cell phone."

"Even when I'm calling about the problems I'm having with the kids?"

"Even then," Taney confirmed. "Though you have to listen to me, too. I'm telling you, Kid, Dani needs to get in a race car, and if you don't put her in one, I will."

Steve laughed, so hard it took him a minute to sober up enough to talk. "You're as bossy as ever, Gideon. I've got a good mind to send her to you for the summer, let you get her started in a quarter midget. Because the problem with Danielle, big brother, is she's exactly like you." He guffawed again.

Taney grinned, ridiculously pleased. He'd also noticed Steve had called him Gideon. "I always liked that girl. I'll take her for the summer, no problems."

Steve gave a low whistle. "Man, you're serious about this family stuff. I can't wait to tell Lisa—when's the wedding?"

Taney held up his hands. "Whoa, buddy, I haven't managed to convince Sandra that I love her yet."

"You're using me as your warm-up," Steve accused.

"Well, yeah."

Steve chuckled. "If I might advise you, oh smart and wise multimillionaire brother who had the brains to start a successful business and then a cup-winning NASCAR team, and yet, who when it comes to women shows every indication of being a total moron…"

"Hurry up and say what you've got to say, so I can hit you," Taney said.

Steve grinned. "You only need three little words when it comes to telling Sandra how you feel."

Taney sighed. "I already screwed up way too much to get away with that."

"Oh, brother." Going by the roll of Steve's eyes, that wasn't an endearment.

"I think I can fix it," Taney said. "I finally figured out what passion is all about."

Steve stuck his fingers in his ears; Taney reached across and yanked them out again. "Not that kind of passion, idiot—I figured that out aeons ago. I mean the kind of passion you and Lisa feel for NASCAR. The love Mom and Dad had for travel. You guys shared stuff with the most important person in your life. It's not about what you love, it's about who you love it with."

Taney had had the time of his life the last few weeks because he'd shared them with Sandra, with the woman he loved. He wanted to be right in there with her, wherever she was, a part of everything, good or bad. A part of her.

"Two things," Steve said. "One, this is way too sappy a conversation for me, and two, you should be telling this to Sandra."

"Just hear me out on one more thing," Taney said. "Then we can go back to your place to see Lisa and the kids. Because I've had a brilliant idea."

Steve signaled for the check. "What's the price of a cup of coffee in Charlotte these days?" he asked.

MACKAY WAS FULLY prepared for Alyssa to sling sharp objects at him as he walked in her door. He hadn't been certain she'd buzz him in, but he'd guessed she wouldn't shrink from confrontation. He told himself he didn't care that he'd blown any chance they might have had of a relationship. She could never have lived up to the excitement she'd given him so far.

He stepped over her threshold with trepidation—the threat of violence, he suspected, was real—and a certain nerve-tingling anticipation. Even facing her righteous fury held more appeal than not seeing her one last time. One last visit for her to say what she thought of him—he owed her that—and then he'd forget about her. Eventually.

He looked for her in the white living room, but she wasn't there. Nor in the kitchen area.

"Well, well, if it isn't my loyal friend MacKay." Her voice came unexpectedly from behind, and he spun to face her.

Alyssa stood in the living room doorway wearing a wrap dress made of a clingy turquoise fabric. It was short as short, of course, but classy and made more so by the large diamond pendant that drew his attention toward her cleavage. As always, she looked stunning. Unexpectedly, she was holding a glass of champagne, raised in an ironic toast. The bottle in her other hand was the finest French stuff.

"Hello, Alyssa." He realized he hadn't planned what to say, he'd been too busy imagining her wrath. Her pleasant smile and the deliberate sway of her hips as she walked over to deposit the champagne bottle on the dining table, next to another flute, were unexpected. He should have known she'd surprise him. How could he have thought she might bore him?

Too late now.

Besides, the art of the deal was being able to walk away.

She held out the second flute, which he took.

"Cheers." The dangerous glitter in Alyssa's eyes sent a thrill through him.

He clinked his glass against hers, took a sip of the chilled, effervescent liquid.

"Your health," he murmured as his eyes ran over her. She was exquisite, and his body tightened just from looking. He would always regret that he hadn't made love with her.

He couldn't remember the last time he'd thought of sex as making love—he shook off the sentiment, and with it the regret.

"Congratulations on your deal with Taney," Alyssa said with menacing neutrality.

"Thanks." MacKay grinned, took another swig of champagne, feeling happier than he had since he'd signed with Taney on Monday. Yes, he should be ashamed of himself and he would be lucky to get out of here with his manhood intact...but sparring with Alyssa was the biggest buzz he knew. "If it's any comfort, Taney didn't give me the deal I wanted."

He had to admire the intransigence of Gideon Taney, who had somehow figured out Lundgren was on his deadline to get a sponsorship in place in time to launch the auto loans business. With Bart Branch already signed, Will was the only half-decent driver available. Lundgren had been forced to yield.

"You knew it would hurt me." For one second, the cool regard was replaced by a hurt so childlike, it gripped MacKay by the throat.

He inclined his head.

"Is that what you wanted?" She was back to detached interest. Dammit, why couldn't she just get mad?

"No, I—" He stopped and fixed her with an uncompromising, level look. "If I hadn't hurt you today, I'd have hurt you tomorrow. Next week. Next year."

She matched his stare, her blue eyes boring into his.

But now, he wasn't so sure about that. Now he felt as if he'd lost something that could have been precious. That maybe he should have looked at the bigger picture.

She smiled, relaxed. "You were scared," she said with satisfaction.

"Don't be stupid."

"There's only one stupid person in this room, MacKay,

darling, and it's not me." With a happy sigh, she took another sip of her champagne.

He had no idea what she was talking about, but she looked so gorgeous, he couldn't wait another second before he touched her. He put down his glass, grabbed her so suddenly her champagne slopped over the edge of her flute.

She made a little sound that was half protest, half pleasure, and she let him—it felt as if she was letting him—kiss her. But it quickly turned, her response fired and MacKay had the upper hand again.

By the time he released her, her blond hair was disheveled, her crimson lipstick smudged. He kept his hands at her waist. He said roughly, "If I was a teenager I'd believe I was in love with you."

It was more than he'd intended to say. More than she'd expected, going by the widening of her eyes beneath her perfect brows.

"I was never interested in teenagers," she said. "Only in real men."

"Real men with money," he amended.

"Of course. Lucky for you." She ran a finger across his lips, and need shuddered through MacKay. She went up on tiptoe and nipped his lower lip, and he groaned aloud.

"Why aren't you angry with me?" he said. "You should have shot me the second I walked through that door."

"I was tempted. But we all have things we fear, MacKay. Possibilities that scare us so much we end up hurting people we—" she eyed him through lowered lashes "—care about."

He combed her hair back into place with his fingers.

"What are you afraid of?" She was probably, he thought, braver than he was.

"The same as you."

"Being poor again?"

She shook her head. "That's only one manifestation. You're afraid of losing something that you've found. And so am I."

He rested his hands on her shoulders. "You are the smartest, sexiest, most beautiful woman I've ever met."

"I'm even smarter than you know." Her smile turned secretive.

MacKay realized he was still running a step behind her—he probably always would be. "Tell me."

"This celebration—" she swept a hand to encompass the champagne bottle and glasses "—is your chance to congratulate me."

She looked so triumphant, he wanted to laugh. Safer to be wary. "What have you done?"

"Like you, I'm now a primary sponsor for a NASCAR driver."

His jaw dropped. "Who? You didn't get to Taney—"

She waved a dismissive hand. "Will Branch will only ever be adequate—I'm sponsoring Brad Stewart."

"But—" he took a step backward "—Stewart is sponsored by Quick Cakes."

"Not anymore," she said. "I had dinner with Larry Preston after the race in Texas." MacKay remembered the way she'd flirted with Preston—he'd thought she was looking for another sugar daddy. "He mentioned that Quick Cakes wanted out."

"Why didn't you tell me you were talking to him?"

She sent him a pitying look. "I knew I couldn't trust you."

He couldn't argue with that. "How much did you pay?"

"I used the same logic that you gave me for Will. Five million this year, six for next year, the option to renegotiate after that. They'd have got more on the open market, but Preston didn't want to advertise the fact his sponsor was pulling out."

"So," he said slowly, "you paid less than I did, with a shorter-term commitment, to sponsor a better driver."

She let out a satisfied sigh. "Exactly." She gave him a peekaboo look from behind her champagne glass and said hopefully, "Are you furious? I know how you hate to pay more than rock-bottom."

She was right. Being done over like that should have him frothing at the mouth. Instead, he let out a shout of laughter, his heart swelling like a balloon.

He planted a hard kiss on her mouth. "Teenager be damned. I'm crazy about you, you scheming, conniving, devious—" he looked down at the amusement in her eyes and his tone changed "—clever, stunning, amazing…" Adjectives failed him, and he kissed her with an intimacy that surpassed anything he'd experienced. "No doubt about it," he said complacently, when he came up for air, "you're the woman for me."

ALYSSA TUGGED his head back down, held back nothing from her kiss. Was this happiness? she wondered. Then she stopped trying to label it and lost herself in MacKay. At some stage, they adjourned to the sofa, made themselves a whole lot more comfortable.

Later, MacKay poured them some more champagne. "You're crazy about me, too," he told her. "Say it."

She hadn't endured his betrayal, the agony of suspense waiting for him to come to her, to make it easy for him now. She shook her head. "I'm not."

Next thing he'd be trying to tell her the elation that burgeoned, the warmth that filled her, was love. But as MacKay had said, that was for teenagers. The kind of teenager she'd never been.

"Liar." He kissed her again, coaxing, commanding. "Come on, sweetheart, say it."

Alyssa smiled with genuine serenity, and shook her head again.

MacKay's frustration was a thing of beauty. His eyes narrowed, his color rose, his fingers tightened around her wrists.

She pushed him a little further, chided him in her bored, sophisticated Alyssa voice. "Really, MacKay, you're deluded."

He saw it for the disguise it was, and he relaxed.

"You're a witch," he said conversationally.

"My, how polite." But she was grateful that he cared too much to use the ruder word. Still, they both knew the truth. "I intend to carry on being a bitch at every opportunity, to you and to everyone else. But you don't need to worry that I'm dumping you," she continued. "I plan on keeping you around."

"Hmm, that's something." He kissed her left temple, then the right. "Why would you do that?"

"Because I find you quite attractive." She taunted him with a quick kiss, her tongue darting into his mouth then out again.

"You're nuts about me," he said complacently.

"You think?" She cocked her head to one side, sucked on one index finger. When she figured she'd driven him wild enough, she said, "You know, there is one thing I adore about you."

His eyes narrowed in calculation—she could see he was already scheming how to take advantage. He leaned forward, nipped her finger. "What is it?"

"Your mother," she said dreamily. "I adore your mother."

He laughed so hard she couldn't help joining in. Laughing wasn't something she'd done much. Still, she'd heard it was good for the complexion, so it might be worth trying more often.

"Let's get this straight," he said. "I'm crazy about you, and you'll keep seeing me because you adore my mother."

She leaned into him, planted a kiss on his firm jaw. "Exactly."

His hand tightened in her hair; he tipped her face up for a swift, hard kiss. "Works for me."

CHAPTER EIGHTEEN

WHEN SANDRA GOT to her father's room on Friday—one of the joys of the Charlotte races was that she got to visit her folks twice a week—she inserted the tape of the Darlington race into the VCR. "You're going to love this one, Dad."

Her father made a vague noise, his eyes fixed on the blank screen. Even when the picture came up, and she made a chivying comment about the race, he seemed less responsive than usual. Maybe, through the fog of his condition, he sensed she could barely speak herself. Sandra sat on the vinyl visitor's chair and let her mind wander against the background noise of cars circling the racetrack.

How long would it take to recover from the hurt of loving Taney, without being loved the same way in return?

She told herself she had the most important things under control. Bart had a new sponsor, and she had appointments next week with a couple of prospective clients who might fill the gap left by Taney Motorsports.

But that still left a gap in her heart.

On the TV, the green light came on and the cars roared over the start line. Her father perked up, his eyes fastened on the bright, moving images.

"Can anyone watch?" Taney's voice from the doorway startled her.

If the thought of him hurt, the sight and the sound of him was much more painful. "Taney, why are you here?"

"Because your office said you were here, and wherever you are is where I want to be."

She ignored that hyperbole. "What do you want?"

"I know the truth," he said obscurely.

"What truth?"

"About Dr. Zakursky." He hunkered down in front of her, put his hands on her knees where her skirt had ridden up. "Sweetheart, I've got this all worked out, so I don't want you to argue with me." He looked serious but the ghost of a grin curved his mouth. "Okay, that's like asking the sun not to shine, but at least say you'll listen first."

"I told you there's nothing more between us." She tried to get up, but he clamped her in place.

"Listen," he ordered. Then, more gently, "I figure you'll want to keep working as long as you can—two years, five years, whatever. I've been doing a bit of reading about this thing, and you can't predict how fast it's going to move."

"Taney, what the—"

He held up a hand. "You're listening, remember?" He winced. "Sorry, sweetheart, I'll try not to use words like *remember* and *forget* lightly from now on. We'll keep going with Taney Motorsports until you can't enjoy the racing anymore, then we'll—"

She pried his hands off her knees, jumped to her feet. "Taney, you are not making a scrap of sense."

He stood, too, so his face was just a few inches away from her, and his eyes were filled with a loving tenderness that took her breath away. "That's another thing—you need to start calling me Gideon. It'll sound weird if my wife calls me Taney—did I mention the getting married part?"

"Taney, if you don't explain what the *hell* you are talking about and how poor Dr. Zakursky got caught up in your ramblings…"

"I know you have Alzheimer's," he said.

"What?"

"I suddenly realized that's why you get so upset by those phone calls from the doctor, why you're so worried." He pulled her into a hug, wrapped his strong arms around her as if he'd never let her go.

"Sweetheart, I love you so much, I don't give a damn how sick you get. I can't lose you now, just because I'm scared I'll lose you later. It has to be all or nothing, like you said, and it's going to be all." He pulled back, looked deep into her eyes. "Sandra, I want to be the first and last person you don't recognize."

Joy bubbled through Sandra, and she buried her head against his neck.

TANEY HELD HER tighter—she was the most precious person in the world to him and he would treasure her forever. Her shoulders shook. "Hush, sweetheart, don't cry, I'm going to make this right."

She lifted her head—and it turned out she was laughing and crying at the same time.

Was this some kind of Alzheimer's response? Hell, he had so much to learn. "Sweetheart…" he said helplessly.

"Let me get this right." She wiped her eyes, beamed at him. "You think I've already got Alzheimer's and you're asking me to marry you."

"I love you," he said. "I don't have a choice."

"And, what, you're going to nurse me when I get sick?"

"As long as I can," he said determinedly.

"Hmm. You know, Taney—Gideon—" his name sounded sweet and strong on her lips "—nurses tend to be patient, even-tempered people. I'm not sure you're cut out for it."

He couldn't help chuckling, and he swatted her behind. "You just watch. And, sweetheart, if you're thinking of making some noble gesture and turning me down—"

"Heck, no." She kissed him hard on the mouth. "If I had Alzheimer's I'd latch on to you so fast you'd wonder what had happened."

"If?" He grasped her shoulders. "You mean, you don't have it?" He saw from her smile that was exactly what she was saying, and it was as if a cloud had lifted and the blue-birds of happiness were twittering overhead.

"Don't you think I'd tell you, if I did?" she said.

"Why would you, when you can't trust me to react the right way?"

"Good point," she said admiringly. She wiped the remains of those tears from her eyes. Taney wished he'd thought to do it for her—he wanted to wipe away every tear she'd ever cry.

"So if it's not Alzheimer's, what's wrong with you?" he demanded, still not sure they were out of the woods.

She sighed. "I told Dr. Zakursky I wanted to do the screening test to see if I have the gene for early-onset Alzheimer's. He wasn't keen, because it's not a terribly reliable predictor, but with so much responsibility in my life, I felt I had to know so I could plan ahead.

"But I kept forgetting the appointment. And then I got to thinking, if I'm that forgetful, maybe Alzheimer's is already setting in, even though I don't think there've been any cases of patients my age."

It was Taney's turn to laugh, and he made the most of it after the tension of the last three days. "It didn't occur to you that you might be forgetting because you're phenomenally busy, you're stressed out and, deep down, you probably don't want to know?"

Her grin turned sheepish. "I just figured that out yesterday. I called Dr. Zakursky, told him what I was thinking, and he said exactly what you did. So I decided not to have the test."

"Good girl," he said, and kissed her. For the first time, the noise of the TV penetrated his consciousness, and he took a look at Sandra's father. "I'd better introduce myself to your dad."

"He won't notice if you don't."

BEMUSED, Sandra watched as Taney approached her father. He shook the older man's unresponsive hand. "Mr. Jacobs, my name's Gideon Taney. I'm in love with your daughter."

Her father looked anxious.

"Gideon, I should warn you, he can be wary of strangers." She loved saying his name—it felt unfamiliar yet resonated deep inside her.

Taney kept a hold of her father's hand. "I want to marry her. I want to help her with that business that wears her out, I want to help her with you and with her mom. But I want much more than that. I want to take care of her for the rest of her life, no matter what."

Sandra smiled, knowing it was true.

"Mr. Jacobs, sir, I'd like your permission to marry your daughter."

The old man's forehead creased in confusion. Then his

gaze flicked back to the TV screen, where a rookie had just put his car into the wall.

"Hooey," he said.

Startled, Gideon turned to Sandra. They both burst out laughing.

"I think that means yes," she said.

"Before I propose to you," he said, "there are a few more things I need to tell you. Since I'm so committed to open and honest relationships."

Sandra listened, amazed and delighted, as he told her he'd visited Steve and Lisa, and they'd agreed Danielle would race a quarter midget this summer under Gideon's supervision.

"That's a great idea," Sandra said.

"That's not all," he said smugly. "I asked Steve to come on board at Taney Motorsports as team manager. I can't believe I didn't think of it before—he's great with the numbers, a strong people manager and he's had years of running his own business."

"And he's nuts about NASCAR."

"Yep. The whole family will move to Charlotte before the start of next season. Jason Kemp will transfer back into All Sports, where he'll be a whole lot more comfortable."

"It's perfect." She kissed him. "Gideon, about MacKay Lundgren…I'll work with him if you want me to." With Gideon beside her, she was strong enough for anything.

His eyes darkened. "I know what that offer cost you, darling, and I appreciate it." His smile turned devilish. "But let me tell you what I did to Lundgren."

She knew, before he said another word, that he'd made things right, and her heart overflowed with love.

"I told him he doesn't get to buy in to the team at a

bargain price. I got him up to eight million this year, ten mil each of the next two years."

Sandra gaped.

"And," Gideon said, "I told him that a large chunk of the extra money will be used to fund a dazzling publicity campaign, to be run by you. I told him he owes you that money—he'll have the most expensive P.R. campaign in town and that's nonnegotiable."

"So," she said slowly, savoring the moment, "MacKay Lundgren will be paying for my parents' care."

He grinned. "I hoped you'd see it that way. What's more, I specified as part of the contract that he can't have any personal involvement in the sponsorship, beyond attending races. Any meetings or negotiations will be with his staff."

Tears sprang to Sandra's eyes. She sniffed. "I can't believe you did all that for me."

"I'm going to spend the rest of my life doing things for you."

She laughed. "I'm sure at some stage I've heard you say 'every man for himself.'"

"From now on, it's me for you and you for me," he said sternly. "Forever. Got it?"

"Got it." She sighed, ecstatic.

"So, is that a yes to getting married?"

She grasped the lapels of his jacket and said, "Gideon, maybe you shouldn't propose until I've had that test with Dr. Zakursky."

"Unless he can also test to see whether you or I will get run over by a bus tomorrow, I'm not interested." He gave her a little shake. "Hurry up and tell me you'll marry me."

"Yes, on one condition."

Gideon waited.

"That if possible, we make this not just a you-and-me deal." She pressed closer. "I want kids, Gideon, and I know you'll be a wonderful father."

He grinned as if she'd handed him happiness on a plate, and tightened his embrace. "You bet we'll have kids." He kissed her temple, then sat down on the vinyl chair, which wobbled beneath his frame.

He pulled Sandra into his lap.

"I'm too big," she protested.

He wrapped his arms around her. "You're perfect. Just stay here forever, and I'll be a happy man." He claimed her lips in what had to be the sweetest kiss she'd ever known.

"I can't wait to marry you," she said, when they surfaced for air. "I can't believe I finally found my sensitive guy."

"You did not," he said, outraged. "I'm the boss of this marriage, and don't you forget it."

Sandra leaned into his strength, gloried in his stubbornness. She could turn this into the first argument of what would doubtlessly be thousands in their life together. But maybe, just this once, she'd go easy on him.

"You're the boss," she agreed.

And tomorrow is another day.

* * * * *

*For more thrill-a-minute romances set against the
exciting backdrop of the NASCAR world, don't miss:
SLINGSHOT MOVES
by Anna Schmidt, available in May
For a sneak peek, just turn the page!*

"I REALIZE WE'VE GOT stuff to work out, but—"

"It's not stuff—it's more complicated than that," Heidi said.

For a moment neither of them said anything, then Steve took her hand in his. "I had an idea," he said quietly. "I'm not sure you'll go along with it but hear me out before you say anything, okay?"

"I'm listening." She forced her clenched fingers to relax and smiled up at Steve. "You've got the green flag," she said.

"It took a while but I think I see where you might be coming from—I mean, why you might think this won't work."

"This being you and me in a marriage," Heidi said and when Steve frowned she held up her hands defensively. "Just trying to clarify," she muttered.

Steve took a deep breath and started again. "I was thinking about what you told me about how things were when you were growing up. Always having to start over— new town, new school, new friends. It finally dawned on me that you think that being on tour will be like reliving that," he said. "So the challenge is to figure out how I can make you see that it's not at all like that."

"Maybe not exactly," Heidi said, "but—"

"No. It's nothing like what you knew as a kid. I can't explain it but I know it's not. Practically everyone I know was raised in a racing family, living that life—travel and all—and nobody feels that way—not the ones who end up racing, building the cars or working on a team and not the women who live on the tour and raise the kids and—"

"And what about those children?" Heidi argued. "What about their schooling and building friendships and—"

"Okay. I'll give you that. A lot of kids today are home-schooled and that's so they can be on the road during the season, but even for those who aren't, there are ways."

"I don't know, Steve." Heidi felt misery surround her. She wanted so much to hear what he was saying and believe in a solution but she knew how it felt. He didn't.

"Honey, I know you're trying to understand and I love you for that. But you've enjoyed the best of all worlds—going to NASCAR events with your uncle and then Kent sometimes but always having that traditional home to come back to, where your mom and dad lived the settled lives of a college professor and his wife."

"So we come from different places."

"You don't get it. If you haven't lived that life—"

"And unless you try the life I'm talking about, you can't fully appreciate what I'm telling you, either," Steve said quietly. "I'm asking you to consider trying something, Heidi—just try it, okay?"

"What?"

"I want you to commit to going to every race with me for the month of May." He held up his hand to stem her protest. "I'd like to point out that two of those weekends are races right here in town—you'd be available should something come up at the clinic."

"Oh, babe, I know I've missed some races but—"

"I'm asking you to take this time to really look at how the NASCAR community works. Hang out in the compound—spend our free time there."

"Hanging out with your family at the speedway?"

He nodded. "In the compound. Mostly at Milo's. That seems to be the gathering place."

"What good would that do? Spotters don't travel in motor coaches or live in the compound. You stay in hotels," she reminded him.

"I just want you to see what it's like. Frankly, I'd love it if you'd agree to move into the coach with Nana and Milo. If not them, then Patsy and Dean have room."

"You've talked to them?"

"Not yet, but—"

"I don't know, Steve. Don't get me wrong. You're family is—fun, generous—"

"Outspoken, overwhelming, chaotic," he added. "It's how we do the family thing. I'm not asking you to change and become like that. I just want you to really look at life on the road—the kids, the spouses, the home life. See for yourself how it works."

Over the time she and Steve had been together, she had naturally been included in any number of family events. But those had all been large multigenerational gatherings where it was easy to get lost in the background. Steve was actually suggesting that she move in with his great grandmother or aunt as if she were a member of the family.

"They scare me," she admitted softly.

Steve burst into laughter and pulled her into his arms.

"Baby, they scare me and I've known them my whole life. But they like you and they think I am one lucky guy to have found you. Believe me, the Grosso women are your biggest fans."

"And if nothing changes?" Heidi asked, her voice shaking slightly.

"Then we'll find another way. On the track you get around obstacles any number of ways—we can do this."

Love Inspired
HISTORICAL
INSPIRATIONAL HISTORICAL ROMANCE

Maddie Norton's life was devoted to her simple yet enduring faith, to good works and to the elderly lady whose companion she was. She believed herself content. But then her mistress's handsome nephew returned home. As she came to know this man better, she began to wonder if two solitary souls might yet find new life—and love—as one.

Look for

Hearts in the Highlands

by

RUTH AXTELL
MORREN

Steeple Hill®

Available April wherever books are sold.

www.SteepleHill.com

LIH82786

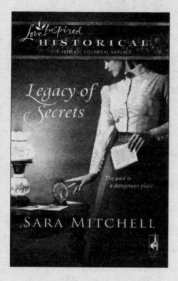

REQUEST YOUR FREE BOOKS!

2 FREE NOVELS PLUS 2 FREE GIFTS!

▼ Silhouette®

SPECIAL EDITION®

Life, Love and Family!

YES! Please send me 2 FREE Silhouette Speäal Edition® novels and my 2 FREE gifts (gifts are worth about $10). After receiving them, if I don't wish to receive any more books, I can return the shipping statement marked "cancel." If I don't cancel, I will receive 6 brand-new novels every month and be billed just $4.24 per book in the U.S. or $4.99 per book in Canada, plus 25¢ shipping and handling per book and applicable taxes, if any*. That's a savings of at least 15% off the cover price! I understand that accepting the 2 free books and gifts places me under no obligation to buy anything. I can always return a shipment and cancel at any time. Even if I never buy another book from Silhouette, the two free books and gifts are mine to keep forever.

235 SDN EEYU   335 SDN EEY6

Name	(PLEASE PRINT)

Address	Apt. #

City	State/Prov.	Zip/Postal Code

Signature (if under 18, a parent or guardian must sign)

Mail to the **Silhouette Reader Service**:
IN U.S.A.: P.O. Box 1867, Buffalo, NY 14240-1867
IN CANADA: P.O. Box 609, Fort Erie, Ontario L2A 5X3

Not valid to current subscribers of Silhouette Speäal Edition books.

Want to try two free books from another line?
Call 1-800-873-8635 or visit www.morefreebooks.com.

* Terms and prices subject to change without notice. N.Y. residents add applicable sales tax. Canadian residents will be charged applicable provinäal taxes and GST. This offer is limited to one order per household. All orders subject to approval. Credit or debit balances in a customer's account(s) may be offset by any other outstanding balance owed by or to the customer. Please allow 4 to 6 weeks for delivery. Offer available while quantities last.

Your Privacy: Silhouette is committed to protecting your privacy. Our Privacy Policy is available online at www.eHarlequin.com or upon request from the Reader Service. From time to time we make our lists of customers available to reputable third parties who may have a product or service of interest to you. If you would prefer we not share your name and address, please check here. ☐

SSE08